Wake's Edge

Pam Withers
AR B.L.: 5.2
Points: 6.0   MG

WAKE'S
EDGE

WAKE'S EDGE

Pam Withers

WALRUS
BOOKS

Text copyright © 2007 by Pam Withers
Walrus Books
A Division of Whitecap Books Ltd.

Edited by Carolyn Bateman
Proofread by Joan Templeton
Cover and interior design by Roberta Batchelor
Cover photograph © picturesbyrob / Alamy
Typeset by Mark Macdonald

Printed and bound in Canada

Library and Archives Canada Cataloguing in Publication

Withers, Pam
    Wake's edge / Pam Withers.
(Take it to the extreme; 7)
ISBN 1-55285-856-1
ISBN 978-1-55285-856-1

    I. Title. II. Series: Withers, Pam Take it to the extreme; 7.
PS8595.I8453W35 2007   jC813'.6   C2006-904980-7

The publisher acknowledges the financial support of the Canada Council
for the Arts, the British Columbia Arts Council, and the Government of
Canada through the Book Publishing Industry Development Program
(BPIDP). Whitecap Books also acknowledges the financial support of the
Province of British Columbia through the Book Publishing Tax Credit.

The inside pages of this book are 100% recycled, processed chlorine-free
paper with 40% post-consumer content. For more information, visit
Markets Initiative's website: www.oldgrowthfree.com.

Dedicated to Layla Haija Hahn

Contents

1   The Houseboat

An ear-piercing scream followed by a heavy splash shattered Jake Evans's sleep. He sat up and blinked in the houseboat cabin's early morning light. He wiped a droplet of water from his face. Then he threw off his covers and scrambled toward the open window. Had he been dreaming or had someone just fallen off the boat's deck into the lake?

He had hardly stuck his sleepy head out the water-streaked window and into the dry Arizona air when someone floating in the water immediately below him swept an armful of water into his face.

"Argh!" Jake shouted as he pulled his head back inside and shook it. Peals of laughter sounded from the lake's surface.

"Ha ha! Got you! Wakey, wakey, old buddy! Nothing like a cannonball into Lake Powell to start your day! Don't you love this desert air and warm water?"

"It's not really that warm, Peter, especially when it's in my face!" Jake moved to the window again and made a face at his best friend, this time ready to duck if Peter Montpetit's muscled arm dared to aim at him again. "You'll pay for that," he added in as threatening a tone as he could muster through a grin. "What time is it, anyway?"

"Breakfast time," called a cheerful female voice from the next window, where the galley kitchen on the three-room boat was located. "Pancakes for our wakeboarders, if you're ready."

"Pancakes? Awesome, Mom. Thanks!" Peter called, breaking into a vigorous stroke toward the houseboat's ladder.

"Yeah, thanks, Mrs. Montpetit," Jake called, reaching for his wetsuit, then deciding he should probably wear real clothes to breakfast.

"A Lake Powell five-star breakfast." Peter's tall, elegant mother was wearing her flight-attendant smile and gesturing to the glassy, canyon-rimmed lake outside. Her blonde hair was perfectly coiffed and she wore white jeans and a silk blouse. As she moved plates of steaming pancakes and bacon to the table, Jake's mouth watered.

She smiled at Jake. "Way better than General Powell got when he came here in 1869," she said.

"Darling, Lake Powell didn't exist then," Mr.

Montpetit corrected his wife. "This lake was part of the Colorado River before Glen Canyon Dam flooded it in the sixties. Mmm, those pancakes smell wonderful. Just the thing for growing boys."

"Dad, we're fifteen, not 'growing boys,'" Peter corrected his father as his fork attacked a tall stack of golden hotcakes.

"Thanks for having me on your spring break vacation," Jake offered politely as he dribbled syrup on his stack. "I've never been to Arizona before. Never been on a houseboat, either."

"Well, it'll do for three days," Mr. Montpetit said with a grin as he folded his newspaper away. "Though I doubt you boys will end up spending much time aboard this boat, what with all the wakeboarding around here."

Jake had a forkful of bacon halfway to his mouth when the sound of a powerboat and a blast of heavy metal music jerked everyone's head toward the window.

"Rock on with Rocky!" said a booming voice over the same sound system delivering the music at high decibels.

Jake and Peter craned their necks to look out the window. Jake gawked at the shiny white powerboat that had pulled up near their houseboat. A buff-looking guy in his twenties with a red bandanna over an unruly mop of shoulder-length blond hair was jiving to the music. A golden retriever with a matching bandanna around his neck sat alertly in the passenger seat.

Jake turned to see Mrs. Montpetit cover her ears and Mr. Montpetit smile and shake his head.

"Sign up now with the rockingest wakeboard school on Powell. Big air, big wake! Let the Wakeup Wakeboard School show you a good time!"

The man paused and grinned at his stunned audience. His golden retriever lifted its paws to the dashboard and barked its own greeting.

"Sweet boat," Peter murmured. "A tournament quality V-drive. Maybe 300 horsepower. Chrome speaker towers and four-board racks. Those are like $60,000. Who is this guy?"

"And check out his board," Jake said, also in a low voice, as he stared at the super-fancy wakeboard complete with sponsor stickers.

"His name is Rocky Benson," Mr. Montpetit said, lifting a cup of coffee. "Better known around here as The Party Animal. A rich, spoiled brat and amazing wakeboarder who gives lessons. A major hit with the kids on the lake. Or so Joe Friesen told me last night when we were at the Beach Pub. Looks to me like he wants you boys to sign up. His marketing isn't very subtle, is it?"

Jake smiled at the boat owner, prompting Rocky to lift his designer shades for a moment and wink at the boys. The man leaned coolly against his boat's chrome tower, the arch over the boat. Wakeboard towers, Jake knew, give wakeboarders' tow ropes extra lift, making for a better ride and more boost. But mostly only pros can afford them.

"Dudes!" the megaphone blared as Rocky drew his boat a little closer. "Me and Hoochie here"—the dog wagged his tail—"would be stoked if you'd like to join us. We're the happeningest school on the lake, and you look ready to hit it."

His eyes were on their boards, which were strapped to a rack on the deck.

"Can we?" Peter asked his father.

"Go ahead," Mr. Montpetit said, fishing his wallet out of his back pocket. "That's what we came here for, right? And don't worry, Jake," he added as Jake began to protest, "this is my treat."

"Thanks!" Jake said, hardly able to believe it.

Thirty minutes later, Rocky gave the boys a helping arm over to his Malibu, which Jake noticed was named "Hoochie's Ride."

"You named your boat after your dog, and your dog after a wakeboard trick?" Jake asked, smiling as he stowed his wakeboard on the tower's board rack.

"You got it! Hoochie and me are hardcore, aren't we, fellow?" His big hand patted the dog's head fondly. "Where you boys from?"

"Seattle," Peter replied.

"And I'm from Canada, just north of Seattle in British Columbia," Jake added.

"No kidding!" Rocky stared at each of them in turn. "I'm from near Bellingham, Washington."

"That's not far from Seattle," Peter spoke up. "So where do you wakeboard up there? Or is this where you live now?"

"Oh, Lake Powell's the place," Rocky said, spinning his boat around and waving casually at Peter's parents as they took off. "But I'm heading back to Eagle Lake for good next month. Gonna start up a wakeboard school there. I think the area's ready for it. Gettin' to be lots of good wakeboarders in the Northwest."

"Eagle Lake," Peter mused. "Isn't that a bird-protection place near Bellingham?"

Rocky's scoff could be heard even over the revs on his engine. "Bird sanctuary, my foot. It's got a lot of birds, for sure—right, Hootchie?" Rocky reached over to scratch his dog's ears. "He loves chasin' 'em."

Hootchie barked in agreement. Jake rested his hand on the friendly dog's back. He had heard of Eagle Lake, too. It was supposed to be big, pretty, and unspoiled. But he'd heard it was all private, owned by some family who used to run a sawmill there.

"That'd be a cool place to wakeboard," Jake said. "Isn't it like five miles long? Wakeboarders are always saying they wish they could get on that lake. So you have access to it? And you're starting a wakeboard school?"

"Access?" Rocky threw back his head and laughed. "I own it! It was my parents' land. When they died last year, I got half, and my sister got half. So yes, I'm gonna move back there now, and it's gonna be the rockingest wakeboard scene in the Northwest. Rocky Benson's good times move north! That lake and its birds sure won't know what hit them, right Hoochie?" He cut his throttle and started to fill his ballast. He threw Jake a life jacket.

"Okay boys, here's the tow rope; start rollin' it out. Get ready to shred some wake and show me your best tricks!"

"Alright!" Jake replied, jumping up and grabbing his board.

Rocky threw the rope into the lake, then jumped into the driver's seat and set the cruise control.

"Show him how it's done, Jake," Peter encouraged as he slapped Jake's back. Then Peter leaned closer to his ear as Jake got ready to climb out over the stern to the boat's swim step. "Like, really show him, so he'll hire us as junior guides for that school of his over summer vacation."

Jake stared at Peter for a moment, then smiled. They high-fived as Jake leapt overboard off the swim step and sank in the water.

2   Summer Job

The water was a bit chilly and milky green, in stunning contrast to the bare orange bluffs that ran ruggedly along shore and the brilliant blue sky overhead. And yet, all three colors somehow swirled and sparkled together in places.

Lake Powell, Jake mused as he brought his knees halfway to his chest and wriggled his toes in the open-toe boots fixed to his board. Perfect glass for 186 miles, snaking into and out of ninety-six major canyons. No wonder it was a world-famous water-sports destination. Nice for him and Peter that this was before the big tourist season; they had peace, quiet, and seemingly endless tracts of water, or what wakeboarders call "butter," to themselves.

Jake took a deep breath of the sagebrush-scented desert air as he pulled the handle of the tow rope to his submerged chest. Rocky was watching him, waiting for the signal. Waiting to idle forward until the tow rope between the tower and the handle in Jake's hands pulled taut and drew Jake from where he hung in the water. Takeoffs could be tricky. They could be embarrassing. They could pitch a person forward face-first into the water. Jake needed to show Rocky he could rise out of the water with grace, balance, and a smile.

"Ready, dude?" came the shout.

Jake gave him a nod and shouted, "Hit it!"

Vroom, vroom. The powerful boat inched forward at just the right pace of acceleration. Rocky was at the controls, head craned to keep an eye on Jake. Peter, who had evicted Hoochie to sit in the front passenger seat, had his eyes glued on Jake, too. Every wakeboard boat was required to have a spotter on board, so the driver could concentrate on driving. Hoochie sniffed the air from a back seat like a statuesque ship's figurehead.

Jake applied pressure to his legs to sink the tail of his board under his body and turn its nose forward. Ready, he thought. As the boat drew away, the rope tightened until Jake felt himself pop to the surface. Knees bent, arms straight, shoulders back, he kept a lock grip on the handle, which he held low to his front hip.

There! He was gliding, smooth as a champion, ready to contemplate a string of tricks. He moved the board back and forth inside the boat's wake, warming up. A little pressure on the toes, a little lift on the heels. Amazing what subtle body movements could do. Just like skateboarding, just like snowboarding. He felt as fluid as the water, happy to be on the lake before Peter, and determined to impress this Rocky guy.

He guessed the Malibu to be doing just under twenty-five miles an hour. Perfect. With a flick of his feet, he traveled away from the wake, digging his toes in. At about ten feet away, he turned and glided back, coming into the spine of water heelside. As his board topped the miniature peak, he paused for effect and smiled. King of the Hill, the oldest game in the world. Now he edged on his toeside and set the board to dancing, up and over, back and over, like a handsaw trying to slice a log. Relaxing, he performed one ollie after another. As Rocky slowed a little, Jake let go of his toe rope's handle with one hand and slowly twirled his board and body around, riding entirely backwards at one point, a one-handed grip behind the small of his back. He resumed his two-handed grip after the surface-360.

He saw Rocky's approving nod and Peter's smile. He felt his energy rise. He snaked left and right like a slalom skier. Then Rocky sped up again, and the little wake rose, spitting whitewater at Jake's knees as the edge of his board played in its froth. He could almost feel the fins reverberating beneath his board.

As a group of kids on a nearby dock gathered to watch, Jake crossed over the first roller and followed the second one toward the wake. Pushing off the top of the swell where the third merged with the wake, he launched into the air. His heart pounding, his eyes on the water, he sought the downslope of the far wake on which he must land, knees bent and backside all but skimming the water, to avoid a crushing impact.

Yes! In a trail of spray, he completed his double-up to cheers from the dock and the boat.

For half an hour, he wove, spun, hopped, and jumped, until his legs and arms were so played out, he slipped and fell on a sketchy landing. He let go of his grip, which skimmed the water as it madly followed the boat. He smiled as he bobbed to the surface.

"I'm finished," he said as Rocky circled around and cut the motor beside him.

"About time," Peter said. "Wondered if I was ever going to get on the water."

"That was awesome, Jake," Rocky said, extending his hand to help Jake onto the swim step. "Good technique. You've been doing this awhile."

Jake laughed as Hoochie lunged forward to lick his face.

"Hoochie, boy, no kissing the customers," Rocky scolded his retriever.

Peter was quick to set up and slip into the water, and quick to one-up Jake with a series of grabs and inverts.

Jake watched, content to feel the desert breeze on his bare back as he spotted for his ever-exuberant friend, who had a much more show-off personality.

"Your friend's been doing this awhile, too, hey?"

"Oh yeah," Jake said. "And he's a little gutsier than me."

"So what other sports do you guys do?" Rocky asked, wincing at Peter's near spill after he'd caught an edge.

"Whitewater kayaking, skiing and snowboarding, downhill mountain biking, and skateboarding," Jake began.

"Skateboarding and snowboarding sure help with wakeboarding moves," Rocky said, nodding.

"Yeah, we were even stuntboys in a skateboarding movie once," Jake boasted, pleased when Rocky's eyebrows shot up at that. "And we've done surfing and climbing and motocross," Jake finished.

"No way! How would you have done all that?" Rocky exclaimed.

"We work as junior guides for an outdoor adventure company."

Rocky, as if forgetting that he had Peter on a line, let up on the throttle and stared at Jake, jaw hanging.

"Oops. Peter just fell," Jake informed Rocky.

But Rocky continued to gaze at Jake for a second. "Can I buy you boys lunch at Powell Grill?" he finally asked. "I'll give you a ride there in my Hummer."

Half an hour later, feeling bronzed and pumped, the boys found themselves being seated in a trendy restaurant decorated with photos of wakeboarders. Jake identified Rocky getting big air in a bunch of them.

"Hey, it's Rocky!" a skinny waitress with long blonde hair greeted them, gushing like a groupie greeting a rock star. "Let me show you to your table."

At least five people greeted Rocky on the way through the restaurant, Jake noticed. Like Rocky, they were all well tanned and wearing designer clothes that showed off their muscles. The smell of charbroiled burgers made Jake lick his lips.

"Oops, better find me a different table today, Janithra," Rocky suggested, hesitating. Jake followed Rocky's eyes to two men in park ranger uniforms drinking coffee near an empty booth toward which Janithra seemed to be headed.

This prompted Janithra to giggle and steer them in a different direction. "Oh yeah, the dynamite incident," she said. "That's no way to fish, Rocky, you wild man. It's not en-vi-ron-ment-ally friendly." She pronounced the word slowly and sarcastically. Jake and Peter exchanged looks. Okay, a guy who drives a Hummer and tosses sticks of dynamite into a state park lake to blow fish out of the water is definitely not an environmentalist, Jake decided.

"A triple cheeseburger for me," Rocky said the moment they were seated. "And whatever these boys want."

He's also definitely not a vegetarian, Jake mused.

"So boys, I'm gonna get right down to business," Rocky said, winking at Janithra before she left with their orders.

"I need some instructors at my new wakeboarding school. And I'd be willing to pay good money and put you up in a cabin if you'd like to spend your summer on Eagle Lake. I'll also tell your parents whatever they need to hear for them to give you permission. All food included, and you'll have access to my Jet Skis, wakeboards, and V-drive."

Peter let go a low whistle. Jake's heart did a happy 360.

3   Eagle Lake

Peter gazed out the window of the bus as it pulled into Bellingham. The little bus station was squeezed between a greasy-spoon café and an empty lot on whose fencing someone had hung a giant, hand-painted sign that read, "Weatherproof fence posts—cheapest prices anywhere!"

"There he is," Peter declared to Jake, pointing to Rocky lying on the grass in front of the bus station with his head on Hoochie's stomach.

"Nice pillow," Jake chuckled.

Peter watched Rocky sit up as the bus driver opened the doors. Hoochie leapt up, tail wagging.

"Hey, Rocky. Hey, Hoochie boy," Peter greeted them, patting the dog as he eased his heavy backpack off his shoulders and leaned on his wakeboard.

"Welcome, boys! So, school let out only yesterday? No break for the wicked!"

"Guess not," Peter said, hoping they'd made the right decision. His parents had assured him that if things didn't work out, they'd be down to pick the boys up in a flash. Knowing they weren't far away made him less nervous about taking a job with this guy they hardly knew. But really, how could things not work out on a private lake with a "Party Animal" fun-guy, lots of wakeboard time, and very cool toys?

"Well, step on into the van. The lake's less than an hour's drive," Rocky informed them.

"Yeah? Where's the Hummer?" Peter asked as he and Jake hoisted their packs and boards into the rear seat of a slightly beat-up Volkswagen van. Rocky cranked up some heavy metal on the radio.

"Sold it. Needed the money. Turns out it costs a bunch to start up a wakeboard school here."

Peter looked at Jake. What was that supposed to mean? That Rocky had run through his family inheritance in Arizona? Maybe his real reason for moving back to Washington was 'cause the land was all he had left?

"Still got Hoochie's Ride and some Jet Skis?" Peter asked as Rocky turned the van onto a dirt road. The dog lifted his head at the mention of his name.

"Of course. What else would we tow our students with?" Rocky's voice was casual and unworried to Peter's ear.

"The Jet Skis are strong enough to tow wake-boards?" Jake asked as the van bumped along the increasingly rutted road.

"You bet, even over sliders and kickers," Rocky replied. "Of course, mostly we use the Malibu."

"You have sliders and jumps?" Peter asked. He could get into speeding up and over a ramp, or grinding his board along a rail sticking up out of a lake.

Rocky grinned and turned halfway around. "Soon. That'll be one of your jobs. Buildin' 'em, I mean."

"Oh."

The road had come to a 'T' at the shore of a long, oval-shaped lake heavily fringed by tall cedars. At one end, roughly three miles away, Peter could see a yellow lodge, a cluster of odd-looking huts or cabins, and a tepee. Smoke curled up from the lodge. He swiveled his head to the other side of the lake. He made out what looked like a dark brown log cabin. Rocky turned on the lakeside road toward the cabin.

"Who lives the other side of the lake?" Jake asked.

"A hippie commune. You don't want to know anything else." Rocky's face went hard as he said it, and his eyes glued themselves to the road ahead of him.

"What's a hippie?" Jake asked.

"A hippie? You don't know what a hippie is?!" Rocky sounded amused. "A hippie is a tree hugger, an environmentalist, a counterculture geek, a world-peace fanatic, a long-haired society dropout . . ."

"Whoa, that's kind of negative, Rocky, isn't it?" Peter interrupted. "Weren't hippie communes big in the sixties? Groovy tent camps of people who were into peace, love, rock 'n' roll, and flower power?" Peter's imagination flashed images of long-haired guys doing drugs, women in flowery frocks tending herb gardens, and naked children running wild. There'd be guitars and harps and beaded curtains and a guru leader in flowing robes . . .

"I said you don't want to know!" Rocky's voice was firm but not angry. Peter felt Jake poke him in the ribs. That meant he was supposed to shut up. Okay, he could shut up. For now. But this lake might be more interesting than he'd imagined. He saw Jake squinting toward the hippie settlement. Peter shifted his eyes ahead.

He could now make out a one-storey log structure with sagging wraparound porch, fronted by a dock. Rocky's boat was tied up at the dock, half blocking the view of a dilapidated boathouse, a tilting outhouse, and a small, faded barn. As they drew closer, Peter saw that someone had recently sawn a square and fitted a window into the rough-hewn sides of the barn.

Rocky switched off the radio's deafening music. The van's brakes squeaked to a halt.

"Well, here we are, dudes," he announced as Hoochie barked. "Toss your stuff into the barn, then come on into the house."

"The barn?" Jake spoke up, glancing from Peter to the drafty-looking storage building.

"You bet. I've converted it into your quarters. Well, almost, anyway. You guys can help finish it up."

Rocky hopped out, lifted some bags from the van, and climbed the steps to the cabin, Hoochie at his heels. Peter looked at Jake and shrugged. He grabbed his backpack and moved toward the barn. He pushed open the door, scrunched up his nose, and stared.

"Mouse!" Jake said as something small and grey scurried across the worn floor of the place and disappeared through a hole lit by the daylight outside.

"A mouse for sure," Peter agreed. "Can you believe the smell? What used to live in here, pigs?" It smelled of wet hay and dust and, well, some kind of animal.

Traces of straw were scattered about the dank, stained floorboards, on which stood a rusty bunk bed and a chest of drawers in need of paint. A ladder led to the barn's loft, where a pile of two-by-fours was heaped beside a toolbox. A faucet that had probably filled an animal trough most of its life was now situated over an enamel bowl resting on a small table. Peter scratched his chin, then threw his gear onto the upper bunk, which sent a cloud of sawdust into the air.

"Whatdoyathink?" he asked Jake.

Jake frowned and looked from the bed to the loft to the window. He went to the dresser, wrestled open the top drawer, and pulled out some pillows. He smelled them and wrinkled his nose. "Not what we expected."

"Yeah, and bummer about the Hummer. Bet he sold it to pay us, assuming he's really going to pay us. You think?" Peter was hoping Jake would disagree.

Jake sighed and tossed his belongings on the lower bunk. "Hummers are gas hogs. Bad for the environment. Better he's rid of it."

"What?!" Peter cried. Of course they were gas hogs, but more important, they were expensive and cool. Right?

Jake shrugged. "Anyway, let's give it a few days. And let's go ask for some mouse traps. Or mouse poison."

"Mouse poison?" Rocky echoed a few minutes later, shaking his head. "What, you want to make Hoochie sick? Nah, just stuff some rags in those holes and keep food out of there. You'll be fine. Want a tour of the property before we hit the water?"

"Sure," Peter replied.

"Okay, soon as you help me put these groceries away," Rocky said, gesturing to the old-fashioned refrigerator in the corner of the four-room cabin. The place was filled with dated but comfortable-looking furniture, half of which was covered with sheets. Rocky opened up some bare, dusty cupboards. "I grew up here, you know." He grabbed an armload of dog food cans and began stacking them onto shelves.

"So, this is where your parents lived?" Peter asked. If Rocky's parents had died a year ago and Rocky had been in Arizona since, it explained the dust and old-fashioned furnishings. Didn't look like his parents had been rich, though. He remembered Rocky telling them they died in a car crash.

Peter watched as a look of sadness passed like a shadow over the young man's face. "Well, yeah, before . . ." He paused and then seemed to recover his exuberance. "But now it's mine. It's also the new head-quarters for the Wakeup Wakeboard School." Rocky grinned as if they should be impressed.

Peter studied Jake wetting a cloth at the sink and wiping out a cupboard.

"Right," Peter said. He reached into the nearest grocery bag. He found doughnuts, potato chips, frozen burritos, licorice, milk, hot dogs, Frosted Flakes, instant macaroni and cheese, ketchup, cola, and sausages.

"Mmm," he said, "can we have some doughnuts?"

"Of course! You're my junior instructors! Eat what-ever you like, anytime!"

The "tour" ran them through the neglected-looking rooms of the cabin, the cobwebby boathouse, and some sheds. "You'll find the brooms and shovels in here," Rocky said, opening one of the sheds.

Jake poked his head in and sneezed.

"So where will the wakeboard students stay?" Peter asked, peering about the clearing among the tallest trees he'd ever seen. He looked up and spotted a bird's nest high above them that looked big enough to sit in. Had to be an eagle's.

"Just day students to start with," Rocky replied. "I'll pick them up in the van in Bellingham each morning, drop 'em off end of the day."

"Oh." Peter and Jake said it together.

"When do the first kids come?" Peter asked.

Rocky shrugged and whistled for Hoochie. "Couple of days, I guess."

Peter snuck a look at Jake, and found Jake looking at him. *I guess?*

"Remind me next time we're in Bellingham to pick up some fence posts and wire fencing so I can build a little yard for Hoochie behind the cabin. For when we don't want him wandering around loose."

"Hey, there was a sign next to the bus station about fence posts," Peter informed him. "Had a cell number on it."

"Perfect. Thanks, Peter. I'll swing past there tomorrow. So, you two ready to get your boards wet?"

"Definitely!" Peter responded.

"Totally ready," Jake said.

"Then grab the canoe from the boathouse."

"Huh?" Peter asked, glancing at the old fiberglass canoe in the boathouse. It didn't look like it had been touched in years.

As it turned out, Rocky had a plan for that old canoe. Peter figured it out as the man had them haul it to a finger of land sticking out into the lake. He had them plant it upside down in the mud just off the spit so that only its bottom showed above the water. A perfect slider, sure to make a wakeboarder as happy as a skateboarder with a rail to grind.

Peter had tried rails only a couple of times on his wakeboard, but hey, no one was around to see him do face plants, and how else was he going to learn? Rocky fired up the boat, Jake and Hoochie jumped aboard, and they were off. Peter went first, and he warmed up with lots of wake-to-wake jumps and grabs, and a few spins. But he knew Rocky was waiting for him to jab a thumb toward the overturned canoe. Only a guy like Rocky, he reflected, would treat a perfectly good canoe like this, but what the heck.

First pass, he chickened out. Second pass, he thought he had it but missed. Third time, he managed to hop atop it and waver for a few feet before falling off like a gymnast trying a balance beam for the first time. But he felt stoked that he'd gotten up on it and was determined to grind the entire length and land his board on the other side the very next try.

Rocky circled around and gave his powerboat some throttle. Peter traced an arc through the clean, blue water as he followed, trying to rally both speed and nerve. He didn't like how sweaty his hands felt. Was it the water or him? He didn't like how the old canoe's bottom looked a bit warped. And he didn't like how his knees sent little prickles of electricity up his legs as he sped toward his target.

Oh, he made the leap up onto the canoe, alright. And he managed to skid along its full length this time. But his board's edge caught as he hit the water, and he ended up toppling in like a falling drunk—a drunkard who forgot to let go of the rope for a second and got tumble-dragged through the water. What he liked least of all, however, was surfacing with a mud-spattered face just off the next muddy spit, and finding a pair of feet planted in front of him.

Slowly, Peter raised his head to take in a girl his age. She was covering her mouth in an attempt to hide a giggle. Her blonde hair was done in dreadlocks, but a few energetic strands had snuck out of place. She was wearing a free-flowing skirt, a bright pink sweater that looked as if she'd knit it herself, and earthy sandals. A henna tattoo down one forearm seemed to point to a hemp bracelet, and she had enough metal bits piercing her eyebrows and ears to set off an entire airport of metal detectors.

"Hi," she said, extending her hand to help him up. "I'm Karma."

4   Karma

Jake had spotted the girl even before Peter did his spectacular face plant into the shallow, muddy bay the other side of the canoe.

"Someone's here!" he'd alerted Rocky.

Rocky, concentrating on driving his boat, hadn't followed Jake's pointing finger until Peter had let go of the rope.

"Hey!" he'd said with a grin. "Karma's biked over to visit!"

"Karma?" Jake had echoed warily. What kind of name was that? Oh, of course, the hippie commune.

"My niece," Rocky explained, looking up and down the treed shore as if checking whether anyone had come with Karma. "She's okay. Okay for a save-the-world vegetarian, anyway."

"Does she wakeboard?" Jake asked as Rocky steered toward Peter and Karma.

Rocky laughed. "That'll be the day! Anything with motors or noise, you know, is anti-en-vi-ron-mental. Or maybe just mental," he added, roaring at his own joke. Then he looked more thoughtful. "If she ever got away from her mom, though," he added, eyes squinting, "there'd be a chance."

"Uncle Rocky!" Karma greeted Rocky with a wave when they came within earshot of each other. "Race you to the dock!" She turned and climbed onto an ancient three-speed bike leaning against a tree and sped over the ruts of the road at dizzying speed as Peter jogged behind, carrying his board.

Jake watched the girl give Rocky a quick hug as her uncle stepped off the boat, then wrap her arms around Hoochie, who licked her face. Next she stepped back and surveyed Jake and Peter in a quick, sunny glance.

"Karma, these are my friends Jake and Peter from Seattle," Rocky said. Jake decided not to correct Rocky, even if it was only Peter who was from Seattle. But he wondered why Rocky had said "friends" instead of "instructors." "Jake, Peter, this is my niece, Karma. She lives the other side of the lake."

Karma nodded her head and stepped forward boldly to shake their hands. She was deeply tanned and rail-thin but fit-looking, to Jake's eyes. Her blue eyes, below all those metal things, glowed with exuberance. And her easy smile bore a strong resemblance to Rocky's.

"So, does Skye know you're here?" Rocky's voice held an edge for a second, even if his face remained cheerful.

"Of course not," Karma said, tossing her dreadlocks. "Have you really moved here for good, Uncle Rocky?" She swung around and looked at the cabin.

"Sure have. Come on in for a doughnut or something."

Karma laughed a light, musical laugh. "You're such a tease, Uncle Rocky. Like I'd eat a doughnut!"

Rocky chuckled and glanced at the boys before resting a hand on Karma's shoulders and leading the way into the cabin. "Well, we just might have some herbal tea or something. And how about some licorice?"

Over the next half an hour, Jake learned that Karma's mother, Skye, was ten years older than Rocky. She'd run off and married a local logger at age seventeen. Then she'd had Karma just before her husband was killed in a logging accident. So she'd moved back in with her parents and helped raise both Karma and Rocky until Rocky had taken off in his teens.

"That's when Skye moved across the lake and invited a bunch of artists and environmentalists to start her—um, her community," Rocky finished, pronouncing the last word slowly and carefully.

"While you broke Grandma's and Grandpa's hearts by becoming a wakeboard bum," Karma teased him.

"That's your mom's version," Rocky said with a forced smile, as if he'd heard the line before. He turned to Jake and Peter. "A school friend in Bellingham got me into wakeboarding, lent me all the gear and stuff. My sister and I are kind of different."

"Kind of?" Karma echoed, giggling.

"And she thinks I'm a bad influence on Karma."

"You are, and that's why you're my favorite relative!" Karma said enthusiastically. "It's a little boring my side of the lake," she confided to Jake and Peter. "Rocky is where the action is."

"I can believe that," Jake said, then hesitated, hoping he hadn't offended her. "So what's your community, exactly?" He asked it as politely as he could while reaching for a second doughnut. Karma, he'd noticed, had eaten nothing.

"There're fifteen of us. We practise subsistence living," she said, shrugging and making a face that resembled a pout. "That means we grow our own food, compost stuff, and don't waste anything."

"So it really is a hippie commune?" Peter spoke up, prompting a scowl from Rocky. "What?" he addressed Rocky. "That's what you called it."

Karma shot Rocky an amused look, then turned and spoke in a patient tone. "They're not called communes anymore," she said. "They're called 'intentional communities.' I'm supposed to say that we share a belief system."

"Yeah?" Peter asked. "Like what?"

Jake wouldn't have asked like that, even if he did want to know. He noticed Rocky studying the kitchen table as if he was trying to come up with a way to change the subject.

"Love, honesty, patience, and tolerance," she said impatiently, as if reciting something she'd been forced to learn. "Equality and respect for the earth."

"Oh." Peter nodded sagely, which meant he was totally stuck for words.

"Cool," Jake said, hoping he didn't sound too lame.

"And you've come here for a little excitement, if not for the hot dogs we're having for dinner, right?" Rocky teased, tugging one of her dreadlocks and standing up to open a cupboard door.

Karma laughed her tinkling laugh again. "Well, now that you've moved back, I hope it's okay if I come visit sometimes. Not for your food," she said, making a face at Rocky. Then she sighed and said in a lowered tone, "To get away from Forrest."

"Can't blame you for that," Rocky said, then turned to the boys. "That's her mom's fiancé. He's a little bossy, and he likes me even less than my sister Skye does."

Karma nodded, her smile having vanished.

"He's so bossy that some of the community members are leaving. My best friend and her parents just moved into Bellingham. Now I don't have anyone to hang out with."

"You can hang out with us all you want, Karma," Rocky declared. "Especially if you want to give the boys and me a hand. We're spiffin' up the place."

That was news to Jake. Did Rocky think they were slave labor for fix-up jobs, or wakeboard instructors? He shot a look at Peter.

"If Skye or Forrest gives me a hard time about you visiting here, I can handle them," Rocky added.

Jake watched Karma's eyes brighten, then move to the plate of junk food that the three guys had all but finished off.

"Well, I am a little hungry. You won't tell Mom if I eat some licorice, will you?"

"Do we look like licorice police?" Jake spoke up, happy for an excuse to make everyone laugh and wondering what the heck was supposed to be wrong with licorice.

"Okay, thanks," she said, lifting a stick of red licorice to her mouth. "Then I won't tell her what you three were doing with that canoe."

"Like she didn't hear it and watch us through binoculars," Rocky returned, his jaw set and his eyes darkening.

Jake gazed out the cabin's window across the lake. An environmentalists' commune and a wakeboard school sharing the same lake? His eyes rose to the noonday sun, and he decided things were sure to heat up, and soon.

5   Rails and Sliders

"First students are coming tomorrow!" Rocky informed Jake and Peter over breakfast three days later.

"Awesome!" Jake replied, relieved that they'd be spending their days on the water now instead of with hammer, saw, paintbrush, and broom in hand. He looked at his calloused hands and glanced at Peter's, which were covered in blisters. Still, the place looked more lived-in now, and Rocky had worked harder than anyone. They'd built wakeboard racks in the boathouse and painted a sign reading "Wakeup Wakeboard School." They'd constructed one slider and one ramp in the lake so far, replaced loose boards in the dock, and painted the cabin's interior to brighten it up. They'd patched holes in their barn quarters and cleaned it up. They would've built Hoochie's yard except that Rocky couldn't get whoever owned that fence post business to phone him back. What was really great, though, was that Rocky had taken them wakeboarding for a short while each day.

"This is my dream," Rocky had told them yesterday. "To launch the Northwest's best wakeboard school."

"You bet! We'll make it happen," Peter had spoken up. "Everyone will be impressed!"

"Everyone but Skye," Rocky had muttered so quietly under his breath that Jake knew he wasn't supposed to have overheard.

Now Rocky's eyes were on the lake out the window. "How about if I teach one of you to drive Hoochie's Ride so I can wakeboard today?" he asked suddenly.

"Um, not sure we're allowed," Jake replied, but crossed his fingers behind his back.

Rocky laughed. "Seen anyone checking who's allowed to do what up here?"

"Me! I'll drive the Malibu!" Peter shouted.

"Okay, and I'm going to launch off the boathouse roof," Rocky announced.

Jake held back a chuckle. Somehow, he wasn't surprised. Skilled wakeboarders could leap off docks and land their boards on the water as the tow rope drew them forward. Crazy wakeboarders launched off lakeside roofs or picnic tables.

It didn't take long for Rocky to teach Peter the basics of piloting his V-drive, although Hoochie whined at the new arrangements. Soon Rocky was posed on the boathouse roof, feet locked onto his board, triangle in hand, rope slack for the moment. Jake took a deep breath as he sat beside Peter, hoping his buddy wouldn't jerk their boss from his precarious perch so fast that Rocky would get injured.

He needn't have worried. Not only did Rocky leap and land it like an acrobat who did it every day, but he promptly launched into the most impressive set of tricks Jake had seen. He started off with a barrage of tweaked-out grabs and spins.

Half an hour later, after Rocky failed to land a 720 and spilled, Peter cut the motor. They heard applause from shore and looked up. There stood Karma in a brilliant yellow sundress, her dreadlocks pulled back today. She was smiling her animated smile. Beside her was a stern-looking woman wearing worn jeans and jean jacket. A limp blonde ponytail hung down her back; dream-catcher earrings made her look vaguely artsy. She wore no makeup on her weather-worn face. Peter guessed it had to be Karma's mother.

"Don't encourage him, Karma," the woman admonished her clapping daughter. "Hello, Rocky." The tone was loud and cool, if not chilly, Jake decided. "Is that what the boathouse roof is for? And is it safe for these boys to be driving a boat on their own?"

"Hi Karma, Skye. How's it going?" Rocky said from

where he hung in deep water. "Meet you at the dock in a minute."

Peter gave the boat a little too much throttle, causing it to lurch forward. Jake gripped his seat and heard Hoochie's claws skitter. But Peter completed the circle and waited for Rocky to climb aboard and stow his board before handing the driver's seat over to him.

Within minutes, they were bumping softly against the dock. Hoochie leapt out and bounded over to Karma. "Hi guys," Karma greeted them in what sounded to Jake like an overly cheerful voice. "Mom, this is Jake and Peter."

"Nice to meet you," Skye said, hesitating before extending a hand. Jake noticed that her hands were cool but her grip firm. "Karma's been telling me about you. She'd like to have you over for dinner at our community sometime."

She'd like, Jake reflected. Not we. And Karma's mother wasn't even looking at Rocky. "Um, thanks. That'd be nice," Jake replied as Peter nodded.

"Excellent. How about tonight?"

"Yeah, thanks," Jake said, looking from Skye's stern face to Karma's broad grin.

"You bet! Thanks," Peter added.

"Now," Skye continued, "if you three kids don't mind, I have some business with Rocky." She raised her eyes to Rocky for the first time and planted her hands on her hips. Jake noted Rocky's shoulders slump like a teen caught out at something, before he nodded and moved toward the cabin's steps.

"Come on, guys. I want to show you something," Karma said, gesturing toward the forest.

"Take Hoochie with you," Rocky spoke up. "He needs a walk." Then, after a look from his sister, "On his leash."

"The eagles are acting odd, especially this side of the lake," Jake overheard Skye say as she and her brother walked across the porch. Her voice rose. "That boat"—she jabbed a finger toward Hoochie's Ride—"and that dog are messing with their egg-hatching season. And if you think for one minute that Forrest and I are going to let Karma . . ."

"Has Rocky showed you the sawmill yet?" Karma was asking the boys, leading them away from the cabin at a pace that had Jake panting.

"Sawmill?" Peter asked.

"All this land was my great-grandpa's, then my grandpa's," Karma explained, turning at a river that fed into Eagle Lake. With Hoochie tugging on the leash ahead, she jumped from one boulder to another alongside the water, heading upstream. "They ran a sawmill that shut down like twenty years ago."

"And it's still there?" Jake asked, feeling stupid as soon as he'd asked.

"Sure. Kind of falling down and we're not supposed to go there anymore, but it's my favorite place, my secret place to go—or used to be. Haven't been there much the last few months. Rocky and Skye played there when they were kids, too." Her face tightened. "Forrest too."

She paused as Hoochie padded to river's edge and lapped up some water, then lifted his head to bark at some ducks on the other side.

"Shhh, Hoochie. Bad dog. Not supposed to scare the birds."

"So how come you're not allowed to go to this sawmill anymore?" Jake asked, imagining rotted floorboards, rusty saws, and pieces of roof ready to fall on trespassers.

"'Cause Rocky sold it. It was part of his half of the land they got, he and Mom. Rocky needed money, I guess." She shrugged, but Jake could see sadness in her eyes.

"That explains the Hummer and fancy V-drive and year in Arizona?" Peter asked—rudely, Jake thought. They were breathing hard because of Karma's pace. She'd left the river to follow a narrow trail between trees draped in gauzy green Spanish moss.

"I guess. The thing is, Forrest—my mom's new boyfriend, er, fiancé—he wanted to buy it. His dad was manager at the sawmill, under Grandpa. But he didn't have the bucks. So Mom's mad that Rocky sold it. And Forrest is mad he didn't get it. Just in case you were wondering why Mom and Rocky don't get along. Besides being different." She produced a wan smile.

"Is the new owner going to start up the sawmill again?" Jake decided to stick with safe questions.

"Nah. No money in it. He's a rancher. Only cares about the parts of the land he can ranch. I've seen fresh tractor tire marks a coupla times and a pile of fence posts, so I guess he checks up on the place. But hardly ever. That's why I can show it to you."

Squirrels rustled in the fern-thick undergrowth, prompting Hoochie to strain at his leash. Jake noticed that Karma kept a firm grip on that leash. When the trail finally broke unexpectedly into a clearing, Jake drew in his breath.

6   The Sawmill

Before them was a pond, and on its surface floated a cluster of the largest logs Jake had ever seen. Beside the pond stood a long wooden building well past its glory days: a mill as big as a strip mall. It was perched on sturdy log legs and partially walled in by worn wood slats. Its corrugated-tin roof was rusty, and inside was a complicated array of iron wheels, belts, cogs, circular saws as tall as a man, hooks, and shafts. Some of these sat on massive stone footings. Moving closer, Jake smelled rust and oil. His feet padded softly on the ground's coating of sawdust. His ears picked up the gurgle of the river they'd followed earlier. It ran into and out of the still pond.

"Look at that ramp." Peter pointed to an iron-plated wooden access the length of several children's slides. It lead up from the pond to the mill's floor.

"That's where they dragged logs up to be sawed,"

Karma said. "Some of 'em three times as tall as a telephone pole. They weighed like four tons. Hardly any trees like that exist anymore."

Jake took some worn stairs up to where the ramp entered the mill. He tested the timber floor. It felt solid. He tiptoed past two massive round saw blades and stood on what looked like a small train carriage outfitted with mean-looking hooks.

"Chains and winches delivered the logs onto that," Karma continued, "and the dog, operated by the dogger"—she pointed to a sharp metal arch—"would sink into a log like a fish hook, to hold it in place. Then two of the millworkers, called a 'sawyer' and a 'setter,' would signal each other how to set the machines to cut it."

"Guess it was kind of noisy in here?" Jake asked, looking around the long, airy, but silent mill. The way the teeth of the iron cogs all connected with each other reminded him of Lego constructions, or that board game called Mouse Trap.

Jake leapt over to a chain of metal disks, each as thick as a Frisbee. "That's the tilt table," Karma spoke up. "If you were a freshly cut board, you'd be rolled off there by the steam cylinder underneath."

Jake jumped off in a hurry, his hands avoiding the metal hooks and chains that seemed to hang everywhere.

"Then you'd be pulled to the trim saw, which cut the wood to length. After that it was sorted, bundled up, and carried to the train cars that ran along that track over there."

Jake and Peter swiveled their heads to where rusty iron rails were barely visible beneath weeds and a tangle of blackberry bushes.

She grinned mischievously. "All I'd have to do is pull down on this lever to get things happening," she declared, resting her hand on a big lever on the wall.

"Yeah, right," Jake laughed, not sure if she was joking. "This place is sweet. Like something that should be made into a museum or something."

"But then we couldn't come here," Karma objected. "Want to see my favorite hiding place?"

"Sure!" Jake responded.

They followed her and Hoochie down beneath the mill's floor, where the heaviest machinery was located. It was cool and inviting down here, a catacomb of hiding places, some of them very dark. They wound and ducked their way between massive wheels connected by belts the size of hammocks. Antique oil cans and buckets were scattered about as if everyone had left without a backwards glance when the last whistle had blown. Finally, just beyond a musty shed at one corner of the mill's underbelly, they followed Karma and the sniffing dog along the top of a fallen log hidden by tall grass.

"In there," Karma whispered, as they came to a low, barracks-style structure of rotting wood.

"Why are we whispering?" Jake asked. He tiptoed after Hoochie's wagging tail down some sketchy rotted stairs, then ducked inside the narrow bunker.

The place wasn't even tall enough to stand in, and some of the floorboards were missing, so it suited Jake just fine to plop down on a blanket that Karma lifted from a trunk in the corner and spread on the floor. Hoochie did a short leap down to the dirt beneath two missing floorboards and began sniffing under there. Karma shrugged and let him.

Lying on his stomach between Karma and Peter, Jake found himself looking out a wide, narrow slat of a window without glass. He watched Karma lift a pair of binoculars down from a hook over the horizontal opening.

"I get it, people shoot ducks from here?" he asked.

"Shoot ducks?" Karma said in a low, hushed, offended tone. "Absolutely not. This is a bird blind. It's for observing wildlife without them seeing you."

"Ah, to take pictures of them or something," Peter suggested.

"Yup."

"Neat. You can see the mill really well, but I sure didn't see this from the mill."

"Yup. Grandpa built this after the mill shut down."

Jake gazed out at the abandoned mill across the pond, which had fallen under a cloud's shadow.

He watched an eagle swoop down on the water and clutch something with its claws. He noticed Karma's hand tighten around Hoochie's leash, even though Hoochie was out of sight in the dark "cellar" beneath them, invisible but for the wagging tip of his tail. The dog's panting below was the only sound in the bird blind.

"That eagle's got a fish," Peter whispered as the eagle flapped mightily to rise from the water with a coho salmon in its grip.

"He's carried it to shore to eat it," Jake whispered back.

The eagle swiveled its regal head back and forth as if checking for danger. It was so close, Jake gasped at its size. He could see almost every feather of the distinctive white head and dark breast. As it bent its strong-looking neck and sharp beak to the coho beneath its yellow claws, Jake wished he had a camera. This was way better than a zoom-lens view in a National Geographic documentary. This was real life, a wild eagle, right up close. Totally magnificent.

"Get a load of that beak," Jake murmured as the eagle ripped into the salmon. "Wouldn't want to be on the other end of it."

Karma giggled softly. "Guess I forget some people don't see them every day."

Peter yawned. "It's a bird, Jake. A bird eating a fish. Whoop-de-do. Let's get back. I'm hungry."

Just then, Hoochie bounded back up from his dark hiding spot, caught sight of the eagle, and barked. The bird's head swiveled around on the thick neck again, and its beady eyes glared at the bird blind. Then it stretched its wings, revealing a wingspan as wide as Jake was tall. With only a couple of flaps, it was away, even before Hoochie yanked his leash out of Karma's hands and shot up the stairs of the shelter.

"Hoochie, no!" Karma shouted in distress.

Three pairs of feet sprinted up the blind's steps and gave chase. Jake caught up with the dog and pounced on his leash just as Hoochie turned over on his back and began to roll in an old, dead, and very smelly fish. The whiff of the salmon hit Jake's nostrils like a slap.

"Hoochie! Yuck!" Karma took the leash from Jake and pinched her fingers over her nose. "Thanks, Jake. Oh no, now he really stinks. What will Mom say?"

Jake thought it was odd that she was more worried about her mom's reaction than Rocky's. Then again, Rocky seemed to love scrubbing his beloved hound in a big tin washing tub on the cabin's porch every few nights as suds floated into the woods-scented air. Almost as much as Hoochie loved his master's attention. In fact, Jake was becoming pretty fond of the affectionate dog, too.

"It's okay," Jake said. "We'll wash Hoochie back at the cabin. In fact, Peter and Hoochie and I will wander back just after you and your mom have left Rocky's if you like."

Karma turned and looked at him with large eyes. The sun glinted off her eyebrows' metal piercings as she smiled. "You'd do that? You understand? My mom can be, well . . ."

"No problem," Jake said. As he backed away from the fish, pulling Hoochie's leash, the sound of the river leading out of the pond made his throat ache for water.

"That river safe to drink from?" he asked. They hadn't brought water bottles.

Karma's blue eyes scanned the old mill's silent, rusty machinery. "Probably not a good idea." She wiped sweat from her brow. "It's warm today, huh?" She inched closer to the pond, well away from Hoochie's fish, and cupped her hands in it to wash her sweaty face. The ends of a few dreadlocks strayed into the pond and disappeared into the shadowy reflections of the mill walls. The ripples distorted the mill's image, made it look dark and foreboding. Jake looked up and shivered despite the heat.

"Thanks for catching Hootchie," Karma was saying. "We'd better get back before Mom guesses where we've been. I get to help make supper for you."

"Sure, let's get moving," Jake agreed, pulling his gaze away from the sawmill.

"Mmm, supper!" Peter added, patting his stomach.

A supper, Jake mused soberly, to which Rocky and Hoochie hadn't been invited. Never mind the commune's so-called belief system of "love, honesty, patience, and tolerance."

7   Hippies

"We have to talk Karma into wakeboarding," Peter declared as the boys, freshly showered, biked along the lake trail toward Karma's community on rusty steeds Rocky had hauled out of a shed. Jake's was a girl's bike with an ugly plastic basket on the front. But better than walking five miles there and then back again, Peter figured.

"I think that'll get her in big trouble," Jake cautioned.

"But she's bored. She said so herself. Can you imagine how bored we'd be if we lived here with no friends, no TV, no computer, not even a phone—except for Forrest's cellphone, which no one else can use? At least we can wakeboard. She said Forrest only lets people there listen to classical music, and hardly ever lets them go into town."

"Thought Skye was the boss of the commune," Jake replied.

"Guess not anymore." Peter shrugged and glanced sideways at the placid lake. He was getting bored already, too. No houses, no people, no stores, nothing up here. Not even a TV in their barn, though Rocky had one in his cabin. Just trees. And birds that woke them up way too early with their sunrise chirping.

Peter felt sorry for Karma. Yesterday she'd told them she'd grown up climbing trees, biking around the lake, swimming, hiking, and canoeing. Anything to get away from the commune and its strict rules. And why else would she be coming 'round every day, bringing the boys and Rocky organic vegetables from her garden and stuff, if she wasn't bored?

"She loved seeing Rocky launch off the roof," Peter said. "She said so herself. I say she has a wild streak in her. It's our job to save her from that boring hippie commune."

"Peter . . ."

"Have you seen her watching us wakeboarding? She's dying to try it."

"I think we should mind our own business, Peter."

"What else is there to do around here besides corrupt a hippie girl?"

"Teach wakeboarding to kids starting tomorrow morning. Read on the dock. Watch the eagles. There's tons of eagles, you know. You should look up once in a while. Listen to the wind blow through the trees. Throw Frisbees for Hoochie."

"Jake, you're joking, right?" But Peter knew his quieter, nature-loving friend wasn't. Which is exactly why he needed to coax Karma to liven things up.

"Hey, this is it," Peter said softly as they drew close to a haphazard array of rough-hewn cabins, lean-tos, tents, and a tepee. These were scattered around a large, odd-shaped yellow lodge under the trees just up from the shoreline. Two massive garden plots filled a clearing on the far side, beside a chicken coop. Closer to the beach sat a ring of rocks and logs around a firepit, from which a wisp of smoke rose to the sky. A pile of fence posts lay near the lodge. Not a soul was in sight. The boys hesitated near the fire ring. Peter wondered whether people roasted marshmallows there, or did weird hippie chants.

He jumped as a gong rang out without warning. Yes, the sound of a padded hammer striking what looked like a giant cymbal suspended from a rope on a wooden frame along the side of the lodge. As he looked closer, Peter saw that the woman striking it was Skye. She must've come out of a rear door in the lodge.

"Jake! Peter!" came Karma's call as she skipped out of the bright yellow dwelling. She stopped, looked at their bikes, and laughed in what Peter had come to think of as a musical tinkle. "Where'd Uncle Rocky come up with those old things?"

Peter felt his neck redden a little. "A shed."

"That one was mine when I was your age," Skye spoke up from where she'd moved toward them. She was wearing a sky-blue sleeveless cotton dress that reached to her ankles, which were decorated with braided string bracelets above her bare feet. A half smile tugged at her face.

"And the dented one was Rocky's when he was a little punk," came a deep male voice from the lodge's doorway as a tall, bearded man appeared. Actually, tall wasn't the word for him, Peter reflected. The guy was well over six feet, bordering on a giant— straight-backed and solid as the trees that surrounded the lake.

His beard reached well down his chest. His thick fingers tugged on its end like he wasn't comfortable wearing it. His moustache disguised any smile he might be trying to project. His eyes squinted at the boys as if sizing them up. He wore an ill-fitting muslin tunic like something from a Shakespearean play, and loose khaki trousers over cheap orange plastic clogs. A jarringly colorful string of beads looped around his neck. Peter had never met hippies before, but his first thought was that this guy needed a better costume consultant. Peter could much more easily picture Forrest running the sawmill than managing a commune.

"I'm Forrest," the man said, extending a hand.

"Peter," Peter replied, as Forrest's sandpaper-rough palm gripped his.

"I'm Jake," Jake spoke up. "We were worried for a minute when we didn't see anyone around."

"We only just finished the afternoon meditation session," Skye explained as she joined Forrest in the doorway. Peter watched Forrest clamp his big hands on her bare arms. Half a dozen adults around Skye's and Forrest's age peered out from behind the couple and smiled hesitantly. They all wore faded sweats or loose-fitting cotton clothes, and most were bare-foot. Except for the occasional nosering or dangling feather earring, they looked more like the participants of a suburban yoga class than exotic hippies. Peter felt mildly disappointed.

"Karma, do you want to show them around until the dinner gong?" Forrest asked her.

The dinner gong, Peter mused as his eyes slid back to the wooden frame holding the gong. He wondered if they changed activities every time it sounded, like kids obeying a school bell.

"Skye, you're going to check on the sweat lodge, remember?"

Skye nodded and walked toward a dome-style collection of branches over which canvas had been hung. Her bare feet produced a soft scrunching noise as she trod on the forest floor's pine cones.

"Attention everyone, these are Karma's friends, Jake and Peter," Forrest boomed out. Peter watched the meditation class folks nod and murmur hellos, but only a few pressed forward to shake the boys' hands. Almost like they thought they needed permission from Forrest to do so. "They'll be joining us for evening social hour."

Peter's eyebrows rose. Social hour? He saw Jake's eyes follow the line of people filing quietly toward the domed structure. Peter turned back toward Karma, if only for fear the commune members would begin to toss off their clothing and enter the sweat lodge naked.

Karma's smirk made him wonder if she could read his mind. "Come on," she gestured, and led them toward the gardens, which were surrounded by tall fence posts and wire mesh. "This," she said in a triumphant voice, "is our organic vegetable plot. We get almost all our food from here. Peas, beans, zucchinis, carrots, herbs, everything!"

"Nice," Peter said, sensing that maybe tending that garden was her big thing.

"And this is our organic flower garden. We sell

flowers in town to pay for supplies. The extra-tall fences are to keep deer out."

Peter was impressed by the ten-foot fence posts and the brilliant colors of the flower garden.

"And everyone here has built their own sleeping spaces." She waved a hand carelessly at the strange cluster of tents and such. Peter liked the tepee best; someone had painted weird bird symbols all over it.

"Up there," Karma suddenly pointed high above them at the branches of a skyscraper-tall tree from which a series of rope ladders hung, "is our eagle observation deck." She waved at a figure on a platform so far up that it made Peter dizzy to try and make him out. "We take turns doing eagle duty."

"That's neat," Jake said, looking as stunned as Peter felt. Eagle duty?

"In there's where we keep the canoe," Karma continued, pointing to a boathouse Peter hadn't noticed before. "I can't take it out without permission," she added with a touch of bitterness. Her eyes traveled back to the lodge's doorway, where Forrest remained standing and staring at them.

"Now I'll show you the main lodge," she said less enthusiastically.

"What's the sweat lodge all about?" Peter asked as they skirted the gardens and campfire circle.

"It's made of twenty-seven willow branches, because that's how many ribs a buffalo has."

"Oh," Peter said. "And it's like a sauna?"

Karma's easy grin surfaced. "Yes, Peter, it's like a sauna. Except it's for spiritual time, not just health. And people wear bathing suits inside it."

"Uh-huh." Peter's eyes scanned the dome warily. There was a pile of clothing outside its door flap. The grounds were quiet except for the twittering of birds. Not a soul was in view except Forrest, still in the doorway, and the guy up on the eagle deck.

Karma marched up the lodge's front steps and right past Forrest without a word. The boys followed suit, Peter nodding to the man, whose eyes continued to bore into them.

Peter blinked as they stepped into an entrance hall. Bright light streamed from skylights high above onto a parquet floor of handcrafted, inlaid wood blocks. Chairs made of bent willow branches were lined up along the sides of the central room, which was dominated by a log table big enough to fill a medieval banquet hall. Pottery vases held an array of fresh flowers.

Peter moved toward a polished cedar carving of an eagle at the far end of the room. It looked real enough to turn its head and stare at him. He reached out to touch the eagle's beak gently.

"That's my mom's. She's a wood carver. Her stuff's in an art gallery in Bellingham. Almost everyone here's an artist or something." Kara pointed to a watercolor painting of Eagle Lake on the wall of the next room. The room's floor was covered with exercise mats. "My friend's mom, the one who just quit and left our community, did that one. Now there's no one my age here." The sadness in her voice made Peter feel sorry for her.

He glanced at the doorway, saw that Forrest had disappeared, and reached into his pants pocket to produce a package of licorice. "For you," he said, ignoring Jake's frown.

She hesitated, looked about, then smiled and reached out to tuck it into a pocket in her dress.

"What kind of artist is Forrest?" Jake asked in a low tone, glancing at the empty front door frame.

"A con artist," Karma said with a sniff, then smirked. "Kidding. He's the one who sells everyone's stuff in town. Makes him think he runs the place," she added darkly and almost in a whisper.

Just then a wiry old man with a tray of steaming-bowls came through some swinging doors. The aroma of lentil soup and fresh-baked bread followed him. Peter heard his own stomach growl.

"Tao, these are my friends Jake and Peter. Tao's our cook," Karma said as she reached out to help the grandfatherly little man place the bowls on the table.

"Pleased to meet you," said Tao, who sported a full Afro of frizzy gray hair. He nodded and disappeared back through the swinging doors.

The gong sounded as he reappeared with a tray of salad bowls. On cue, a silent file of people with glistening faces—and, Peter was relieved to see, their clothing back on—streamed through the rear door.

By the time Jake and Peter had washed their hands in the sink of a large kitchen full of hanging woks and pans, the table was heavy with platters of food Peter couldn't identify. Forrest, sitting at the head of the table, gestured for the boys to sit on either side of him.

"Those are soy burgers," Karma said, as if in answer to Peter's mystified look. "That's cauliflower-cheese casserole, my favorite. You're allowed to dip your oat buns into your lentil soup. And Tao's potato-tofu curry is famous."

Peter didn't need to ask if there were any meat dishes. Rocky would've been making rude comments by now, Peter mused. But Peter was determined to be polite and brave.

He noticed that no one served themselves until Forrest had filled his plate, not even Skye. In fact, hardly anyone spoke. They just smiled passively at the boys between tucking into their dinner. Some social hour, he thought. But he licked his lips as he finished the lentil soup, and he couldn't believe how much his taste buds liked the first forkful of the cauliflower-cheese casserole. Maybe vegetarians were onto something.

"So," Forrest began, as if he'd called a formal meeting. "Are you aware that there are eighteen eagle nests on the two properties around this lake, and this is nesting season?"

"Cool," Peter replied. From the corner of his eye, he saw Karma frown and throw her mother a pleading look. Skye's return glance to her daughter seemed to hold an apology, but her spoon continued to dip into her lentil soup.

"Any disturbances, such as motors or barking dogs, could stress them and impact whether the eaglets hatch."

Peter and Jake nodded, their mouths on fire with spicy curry.

"As I'm sure you know, there's also lots of fuel emitted by those Jet Skis," Forrest continued. "You look like boys who enjoy the outdoors, so I'm sure you'd like to see Eagle Lake stay unpolluted."

"Yes sir," Peter replied, eyes veering to Karma as she pushed her plate away and glared at Forrest.

"Nice place," Jake spoke up. "Very peaceful, and we really like that eagle carving."

"Thanks," said Skye, smiling and placing a gentle hand on Karma's shoulder. She actually looked nice when she smiled, Peter decided.

"How long have you been here?" Peter asked Skye, taking Jake's cue to change the subject. Karma picked up an oatmeal bun and sliced it open with her knife.

"Ten years," Skye said, pride in her voice.

"And you?" Peter addressed Forrest bravely.

Forrest's eyes narrowed. "Six months," he replied, standing and wiping his mouth with his napkin. He rose and walked over to Skye, his body towering over her. "So I'm going to ask you boys to have a conversation with your boss, okay? Out of respect for the eagles, of course."

"I'm not hungry anymore," Karma declared. "Can I take the boys up to the eagle platform now, Mom?"

"You may," Forrest spoke up before Skye could reply, his dark eyes on Peter and Jake. "Just see them off and be back before the evening log circle."

Somehow, Peter didn't want to know what the log circle was about.

Karma's chair screeched as she pushed it back. Peter would've liked seconds or dessert, but he got the message as Jake kicked him under the table. The two rose, thanked Tao, Skye, and Forrest, and excused themselves to the rest of the statues at the table—at least, that's how Peter was beginning to see them.

The fresh evening air was a welcome change from the stuffy dining room, Peter thought. And climbing a series of rope ladders up a tree so high that they needed climbing harnesses that clipped onto a special safety rope was exactly what he'd hoped Karma would let them do.

8   Private Lesson

"**I** can't believe how big eagle eggs are," Jake commented to Peter the next morning over breakfast. He'd loved last night's trip up to the platform, where a telescope was trained on a nest across the forest clearing. The eggs were like goose eggs, twice the size of chicken eggs. "It'd be so cool to see them actually hatch."

"I can't believe how big their nests are either, or that the commune hauled a telescope all the way up to that platform to keep watch on that nest," Peter replied, pouring himself a second bowl of Frosted Flakes.

"Yeah, wonder if the mother and father eagles know they're being spied on 24-7?"

"It's far enough away. They're not disturbing them. Hey, where are the Pop-Tarts?"

"Rocky ate them all. Maybe he'll bring some more with the kids. Or better yet, something healthier.

Speaking of bringing the kids . . ."

The boys looked up as ear-splitting music boomed at them from Rocky's approaching van.

"Our first class! Lucky little devils," Peter said, shoveling spoonfuls of cereal into his mouth as Jake stood and opened the cabin's door.

Jake counted seven kids as they spilled out of the van. All from Bellingham, Rocky had told them, and ages seven to ten. The seven-year-old remained in the van, looking frightened, arms wrapped around himself, face tear-streaked.

"Alright! Welcome to the Wakeup Wakeboard School!" Jake shouted over Hoochie's barking. "You'll all be stars by the end of today," he grinned his best wakeboard-instructor grin.

He helped Rocky unload stuff from the back of the van and directed Peter to help the kids get their life jackets on. He noticed it took Peter a full ten minutes to coax the littlest boy from the van.

"That one's named Dougie," Rocky said. "Too young and timid for this, I think, but his mama paid, so we're stuck with him."

Within half an hour, Rocky, Jake, and Peter had made the kids pick a partner and lined them up along the shore. The pairs—Jake partnered himself with Dougie—practised pulling each other up by the triangular bar on the end of a practice tow rope.

One partner was the pretend boat, and the other the wakeboarder.

"Knees bent halfway to your chest. Grab the handle palms down. Keep that body balanced and arms straight as your partner pulls you up," Rocky coached them.

"Dougie, what's wrong? Don't want to do this?" Jake asked gently.

"Uh-uh," he said, eyes on Hoochie, who was lapping up lake water down at the beach.

Jake grinned as an idea hit him. "Hey Hoochie. Here, boy."

Hoochie turned and bounded up. "Hoochie, this is Dougie. Your new partner."

Dougie grinned. Hoochie pushed his wet nose into the boy's face.

Jake slipped the practice tow rope through Hoochie's collar and pretended it was Hoochie pulling Dougie up. Dougie giggled and started doing the exercise along with the other kids.

For the rest of the morning, Hoochie stuck with Jake and Dougie, keeping the boy's spirits up, chasing the Frisbee that Jake allowed Dougie to toss the dog during breaks, and following the boy when he waded into the water.

"Good boy," Jake told Hoochie, wrapping his own arms around the friendly dog. He could feel Hoochie's heart beating against his palm. The dog's big brown eyes held Jake's as his tail thumped rhythmically on the dock. His golden coat smelled freshly shampooed. Jake hugged the retriever tighter, wishing he had a dog as intelligent and playful as Hoochie. He was beginning to understand how Rocky could be so attached to his hound.

By the afternoon, every one of the students had mastered rising from the lake behind the boat, even Dougie. Some had even advanced to surface 180s, ollies, and riding switch.

The sun sparkled on the water, and the kids pointed as eagles occasionally flew overhead. When Rocky gave Jake and Peter a chance to show off for the kids, Jake basked in the clapping, oohing, and ahing.

"Jake," Dougie said afterwards, tugging on the hem of Jake's wet shorts.

"Yes, Dougie?"

"Why do fish die?"

"Why do fish die?" Jake bent down so he was face-to-face with the shy boy.

Dougie pointed a stubby finger down the beach. Jake took Dougie's hand and walked along the muddy shore to something that had just washed up on the waterline. A dead salmon. He was about to reply when he caught sight of an eagle feeding on a second dead salmon a little further down the shore.

He turned back to Dougie and motioned him back toward the dock. "Fish, animals, people—everyone gets old and dies eventually," Jake explained. "At least when the fish in this lake die, they make a nice meal for the eagles."

Dougie pulled his face into a pout and crossed his arms. Jake tried not to smile.

"Dougie!" Rocky was calling. "Van is leaving!"

Jake reached out to high-five his young student.

"Had fun today," the boy admitted, letting his face break slowly into a beam.

"Awesome," Jake said. "Come on back anytime. Hoochie'll be waiting for you."

Rocky helped Dougie into the van. "You and Peter did a great job today," he said, slapping Jake on the back. "I'll be back in a while. Gotta stop at Bellingham Hardware for fence posts for Hoochie's yard. Whosever cellphone that was advertising cheap fence posts never returned my calls."

The kids' hands waved wildly as Rocky hopped into the driver's seat.

"See you," Jake said, still relishing Rocky's compliment. "Think Karma is coming around today?" She'd been showing up at least once each day, sometimes helping them hammer, sometimes bringing them organic vegetables from the commune's—er, the intentional community's—garden.

"You have to feed your workers better than this, Uncle Rocky, even if you won't eat vegetables yourself," she'd said.

To which Rocky had replied, "We eat vegetables: pickles on our burgers!"

Rocky pulled his sunglasses down from his red bandanna to his eyes. "Will Karma be here? Beats me," he said, leaning out his window. "That girl marches to her own drummer. But I've sure been noticing her watching us board. Like she's dying to try it."

Minutes after the sound of Rocky's van music had faded away, Jake and Peter were flopped down on the dock when they saw a bicycle approaching.

"Hey!" called Karma. "You two are going to get sunburned."

Jake sat up and smiled as she stepped off her bike, leaned it on its kickstand, and sat cross-legged beside them on the dock. She smoothed her sundress. Jake noticed a pair of binoculars hanging around her neck.

"Karma, come for your private lesson?" Peter asked, pointing to the stacked wakeboards near the boathouse. "We're qualified instructors, you know— been warming up for you all day!"

Jake sighed. He didn't like Peter's campaign to get Karma into things that might get her into trouble with her community. Though the truth was, he'd kind of like to see her wakeboard, too. If she wanted to.

Karma smiled at them. "Mom would totally kill me. She says you should be arrested for disturbing the peace of Eagle Lake. Oh, I brought you some free-range eggs and some spinach." She stood and reached for a bundle in the basket of her bike.

"Hey, thanks! They'll go great with our sausages tonight," Jake teased her, prompting Karma to wrinkle her nose. "Free-range chicken eggs, I assume, not eagle eggs."

"Jake! That wasn't funny!"

"You're right. Hey, whose binoculars are those?"

"Mom's."

"So," Peter inserted, "that means she can't see you if you wakeboard today. Unless she's on eagle duty and turns the telescope the wrong way. Or has a second pair of binoculars."

"She's not and she doesn't."

Jake waited, wondering, as he saw Karma's eyebrows arch thoughtfully. She glanced across the lake, then down at her binoculars, then at Rocky's boat.

"Okay, just once," she decided.

"Yes!" Peter responded, punching the air with his fist. Jake had been listening to Peter try to talk her into it for days. Well, Jake sighed to himself, it was her decision. Influenced by Peter, maybe, but hers. And any girl who'd grown up climbing trees and swimming in this lake would probably be a quick learner.

As it turned out, she had a swimming suit on under her sundress, and a towel wrapped around the eggs she'd brought, making Jake wonder if she'd planned it all along.

"You give her the first lesson," Peter said to Jake. "Then I'll show her how it's really done."

Jake pulled out the boards and rope, sat his eager student down on the dock, and went through the basics on shore. Compared with Dougie, she was a pro within ten minutes. Only half an hour later, Peter was in the driver's seat of the powerboat, Jake was spotting, and Karma was in the water waiting to rise. A few tumbles and she had it, grinning ear to ear. Within an hour, she'd mastered all the stuff the kids had taken all day to do. And by the time Rocky had returned, she was halfway to pulling off a heelside wake-to-wake jump.

"Well, well," Rocky boomed as he parked the van. His tanned, smiling face caught the evening's sun. "Peter driving the Malibu without my permission, Karma risking the wrath of Eagle Lake's East Side, and Hoochie lying on the porch like he's been fired as first mate. All of which is okay with me, except for Hoochie's demotion."

Jake laughed as he looked over to see Hoochie lying in the shade on the porch. "We forgot all about him," he said. "Would've let him in the boat if he'd asked. Guess the kids wore him out."

"Looks dead as a doormat to me," Rocky mused. "Not like my niece here. Didn't know you had it in you, Karma. You're making me a proud uncle, although you're definitely not endearing me to your mom."

"I can almost do a wake-to-wake now," Karma replied, giggling. "Want to see me?"

She performed all her new moves, then accepted Rocky's invitation to stay for supper. "Only if I can make you supper," she added. "Spinach omelets with spinach from my garden. Our garden," she corrected herself.

"Sure, the sausages can wait," Rocky ruled.

"So Karma, don't your folks wonder where you are when you're over here?" Jake asked, curious as he helped her rinse and chop up spinach. "Don't you have classes or activities all the time? And what about school?"

"Mom home-schools me," Karma replied, directing her sunny smile at him. "And yes, I've been sneaking out of activities. And getting punished for it." Her eyes flashed defiance. "But they can't stop me from visiting my uncle. Why should they?"

Rocky, stepping in from the porch, scratched his head, winked at her, then set a bowl of dog food down on the kitchen counter with a frown. "Hoochie won't eat," he said.

"That's 'cause he was snacking between meals on a fish he chased an eagle off of, the rascal," Peter reported. "Hey Karma, Rocky bought some chocolate bars in town!" He was rummaging around a grocery sack he'd brought in from the van. "You can eat those, can't you?"

"Yeah, but there's not much nutrition in them," Karma replied, squinting at him. "We don't eat things like that in my community."

"But you're over here, and you can eat what you want," Peter said. "Gotta live a little, hey?"

"Karma!" a woman's voice blared from the beach.

Jake peered out to see Skye drawing up to the dock in the community's canoe.

"You get out here this minute, before Forrest gets here and makes way more of a scene than I'm going to."

Karma's knife froze over the spinach. Her jaw set. Rocky sat down heavily in a kitchen chair out of view of the doorway.

"Up to you, Karma," Rocky said softly, sympathy in his eyes.

Jake started as Karma's knife clattered onto the kitchen counter and she tore out the door. But as she passed the kitchen table, he noticed her hand shoot out and close around one of the chocolate bars Peter had spilled from the grocery bag.

"Bye, Karma," Jake called after her.

9   Weekend Guest

"**Y**ou shot me!" Karma cried out. "I'm bleeding! I'm dying!"

"Yeah, sorry about that," Peter replied with a laugh. "But it's okay. You'll come back to life in a minute, a new person. Can't believe you've never played a video game before."

"We don't have a TV or a computer in our lodge," Karma said, shrugging. "And if we did, Mom sure wouldn't let me play a game with guns in it."

"Which means Peter shouldn't be playing Slaughter-fest with you," Jake spoke up from the cabin's kitchen, where he was stirring the blueberries that Karma had picked that morning into the pancake mix.

"Oh Jake, stop being an old grump," Peter retorted. "Breakfast ready yet?"

Jake frowned but decided not to pick a fight with Peter in front of Karma. Both the boys and Rocky had been amazed when she'd shown up by bike yesterday—Friday—afternoon as they'd been hanging out on Rocky's porch, recovering from the day's wakeboard lessons. A heavy backpack had hung from her shoulders, and fresh vegetables had filled her bike basket.

"Guess what?" she'd said, sweat glistening on her face. "Mom and Forrest made me a deal: I can stay here for the weekend, just this once, if I promise not to sneak over here and miss activities anymore the rest of the summer. Gotta be home Monday morning or else."

"No kidding!" Rocky had said, springing up once the shock had eased off his face. "Well, welcome!"

"Cool," Jake had remarked.

"That's so awesome!" Peter had said, leaping out of his hammock and rushing to help her unload the veggies.

Then, much to Jake's dismay, Peter had proceeded to "hog" Karma to himself, herding Rocky's easygoing niece from one illegal activity to another. Illegal, that is, by her mom's standards. Playing computer games rated eighteen-plus. Watching TV. Making ice cream sundaes smothered in chocolate syrup. Coaxing her to try launching her wakeboard from the dock, then daring her to attempt her first jump up to the slider. She'd fallen, of course, and bruised an arm. Not that she'd seemed much bothered by it, and Rocky had laughed it off.

Why was Peter so into exposing Karma to all the things her community had forbidden? Jake didn't like it, not one bit. He figured it was all going to lead to trouble.

What galled Jake most of all, though, was what Peter had done just before sunset last night. He'd talked Karma into a race on the Jet Skis that had spread the high-pitched screams of the watercraft from one end of the lake to the other. They'd performed U-turns right in front of the commune's beach!

While Rocky had cheered them from the cabin's dock—"You go girl!"—Jake had been forced to cover his ears and shake his head. He wondered what that show of defiance was going to cost her after her weekend was up. Lifting his eyes to the sky, Jake had seen nearby eagles rising from their nests and flapping away. They had eggs to sit on, didn't they? Were Skye and Forrest right about the wakeboard school stressing the eagles, endangering the hatching process?

And what about the dead fish that kept showing up along their shore? The smell made the wakeboarding kids plug their noses and complain, even though Rocky, Jake, and Peter had been picking the fish up with shovels and burying them as fast as they could. Could the fish be dying from all the fuel that the wakeboard school boats were putting out? Not a chance, Rocky had snorted.

"Ha! We just killed the whole division with one grenade!" Karma said, elated. "Die, soldiers, die! Nice teamwork, Peter."

"You've turned evil," Peter objected with a glint.

"Pancakes are ready," Jake reported, proud of the crisp golden hotcakes he was lifting off the grill. "Eat up before Rocky and the kids get here!"

It was a fine Saturday morning, breezy and fresh. Tonight, he and Peter would get their first paychecks. Tomorrow, their first day off, Rocky had promised to take them to a strip of oceanfront beach near Bellingham with a Jet Ski for some ocean wakeboarding. How cool was that? And now Karma could come with them. After breakfast, Jake moved to the dock, took a deep breath of the cedar-scented air, and stuck his toes in the peaceful lake's lapping water.

The peace lasted only minutes before Peter and Karma joined him. "You're all wet!" Peter shouted as his dangling feet kicked water Jake's and Karma's way. Karma's giggle was drowned out by the put-put of Rocky's van, along with high-volume music and children's laughter. Next came the slamming van doors and Rocky's loud hello.

"Want to pull a kid on a Jet Ski this morning?"

Peter asked Karma, even though Jake knew he had no authority to do so.

"Yup!" she said, eyes lighting up. "I can help out! We used to have kids in our community, but those families have left now. Wish I could leave, too." She tossed a stick into the lake. Jake noticed that Hoochie, lying at her feet, didn't bother to plunge in to chase after it.

Jake saw Rocky frown but wasn't sure if it was from Karma's comment or Hoochie's laziness.

"Karma, you get the kids into their life jackets, okay?" Rocky directed. "I'll refuel the Jet Skis."

They divided the kids into four groups and got them going on the basics. Rocky had assigned Karma all the girls, who seemed to take to her like ducklings to a mother duck. How a girl who'd been wakeboarding for less than a week could be an instructor was beyond Jake. But she was only covering the basics, he reminded himself, and she had proven an incredibly quick learner herself. Besides, they were just little kids. And for Rocky, she was a free instructor.

By mid-morning, the more advanced kids were neatly shredding the waves behind Hoochie's Ride. Hoochie himself seemed to have lost interest in his first-mate job. He kept rolling in dead fish Jake hadn't cleaned up yet. Or he watched, muzzle resting on outstretched paws, from the shade of the porch.

Well, it was kind of hot, Jake admitted.

"Rocky," Peter called out, "I promised Karma she could run a Jet Ski while Jake and I got the kids hitched up behind it. Then we can concentrate on coaching 'em. Okay with you?"

She has almost no boat-driving experience and has wakeboarded for only a few days, Jake thought to himself. Not that operating a Jet Ski is brain surgery, but . . .

"Sure, makes sense," Rocky replied, "as long as the older students take turns spotting. You okay with that, Karma?"

"You bet!" She tied one of Rocky's red bandannas around her dreadlocks and hopped onto a Jet Ski. That made two boat operators with blond locks and red kerchiefs. Cowboy Rocky and Cowgirl Karma. Jake couldn't resist a smile when they revved up together like cars about to drag race. Definitely a family resemblance.

Jake and Peter got busy supervising the lineup of students waiting behind Rocky's and Karma's steeds. Vroom went the boats. Up, splat, sink went the students. The boats circled back. Vroom, up, wobble, splat, sink. And eventually, for the more coordinated, vroom, up, sail, snake, leap, land, splat, and sink. Everyone had a little trouble at first, but once they got a feel for getting up on top of the water, they started looking totally comfortable with carving and slashing around. And so it went all day, Peter and Jake taking over the Jet Ski in turns. During a break near the end of the day, Karma turned her students over to the boys. "I'm going to be a student again," she announced as she joined them during a work break on the dock. "Gotta learn some new moves."

"Yes!" Jake encouraged her as he looked up from where he lay on the dock with one hand trailing in the lake.

"Yeah, you're ready for your first inverted trick," Peter agreed, lying on the warm boards with his hands behind his head.

"What's that?" Karma asked with a big smile.

"You've seen figure skaters jump up and spin midair before coming down and landing, right? Or snowboarders doing 360s, a full body spin in the air?" Jake asked her as he sat up.

"Well, sort of . . . in magazines," she replied, still standing over the boys.

"Oh, right. I forgot you don't have TV. Well, same here except the rope's handle makes it a little easier," Jake continued. He rose and grabbed a wakeboard handle. "Stand on the dock like this, holding the handle. Peter, keep the handle tight, okay?"

"No problem," Peter said, rising, taking the end of the practice tow rope in his hands and stepping back.

"Turn your head in the direction you want to turn," Jake continued, nodding as Karma turned her head. "But not till you've pushed off the very top of the wake and are up in the air. That's called flying before buying the move."

"I'm flying," Karma joked, jumping up and down on the dock and turning her head.

"Awesome. Now pull in on the line, keeping it tight. If you start going too fast, open your body and let out the handle. That's it! You're good!"

After she'd practised on the dock lots of times, Jake hopped on the Jet Ski and Peter coached her from the dock as she readied herself behind the tow rope in the water. Jake couldn't believe how fast his own pulse was beating as he waited for her "hit it!" He knew she could fall, probably would fall, while setting up to land. He rubbed his tummy to quiet the butterflies there and hoped she wouldn't hurt herself.

"Hit it!" came the shout from behind.

The Jet Ski's loud whine, the splashes on his face, the vibrations that coursed from the machine through his body: all felt right and relaxed Jake a little. He glanced back just once, in time to see her pop off the wave and look over her left shoulder. Oops! All too soon she was upside down, rotating back toward the water.

He didn't have to turn again to know she'd splatted. He cut the throttle and circled back to where she floated, grinning ear to ear.

"Close," he said as she splashed him with a sweep of her hand. "Not everyone comes that close on their first try."

"I fell on my face over my toes, forward," she giggled.

"It's okay. Just means you need to keep your shoulders back more next time."

"Good effort," Peter called from the dock. "You're gutsy, Karma!"

"Yeah, Karma!" a few kids chorused as they joined Peter on the dock.

"That's my niece," Rocky called out, grinning proudly. "You're gonna have it in no time, girl! Okay kids, that's a day. Last one in the van is an ugly duckling, and you don't want to know what Hoochie does to ugly ducklings, do you?"

Jake smiled and helped the kids as they scurried to return the gear and leap into the van.

Two and a half hours later, when Rocky returned from town, his junior instructors were still played out.

"I'm done for," Karma said, flopping into the hammock on the porch.

Rocky, who was hitching the trailer holding one of the Jet Skis onto his van for the next morning's ocean excursion, beamed. "Hoochie looks done for too, and he hasn't even done anything. How about someone fills his water bowl and fetches everyone lemonade while they're at it?"

"I would, but I don't have the energy to get out of this hammock," Karma said.

Jake was about to rise when a movement out on the lake caught his eye. "Oh no," he said. The others followed his glance to where a canoe with two figures was paddling steadily toward them. In the bow was a slim woman with long blond hair, and in the stern, someone tall and powerful.

"It's not time yet," Karma said as her lips formed a pout.

10   Bundle of Gray

Peter watched Rocky raise his head, study the approaching canoe, then finish tightening the trailer hitch. Slowly, Rocky made his way up the porch steps to wait. It made no sense to Peter that Skye and Forrest were paying them a visit. It was Saturday evening, and Karma wasn't due home till Monday morning. Plus, she had her own bike here.

But one look at Skye's and Forrest's dour faces, and he knew they hadn't traveled over to share a glass of lemonade on Rocky's porch. They looked more like a couple attending a funeral.

As the canoe touched the dock, Skye jumped out lightly and tied it up. Forrest nearly tipped the thing standing up to get out. For someone who'd grown up around here, he sure didn't look like the canoeing type. Then again, it's not like the son of a sawmill manager had access to Eagle Lake without an invitation, Peter figured.

"Good evening, Skye. Long time no see, Forrest." Rocky greeted them as if he was entirely accustomed to canoeists dropping by. Peter had to hand it to his boss. He was trying. His voice was totally friendly, if guarded. Karma, meantime, had sunk so deeply into the hammock that all Peter could see of her was a stray dreadlock dangling over one side.

"Came to show you something, Rocky." Skye's voice was soft but weary. Her bare feet climbed the porch steps noiselessly.

Peter let go of a breath he hadn't realized he'd been holding. At least they weren't going to start yelling at each other right away. Forrest was standing back near the dock, saying nothing, just looking around like a tourist.

Skye held a small bundle in her hands, wrapped in a soft cloth. Peter watched Jake's eyes move to it, and Karma's face lift ever so slightly from the hammock. Skye extended her hands toward Rocky, waiting for him to take the bundle.

Down on the beach, Forrest shifted from one foot to another. High overhead, an eagle's angry warble broke the stillness.

Rocky gazed at his sister, questioning. Skye's steely eyes returned Rocky's stare. Finally, Rocky took the bundle and slowly lifted a flap. Peter's head craned as Rocky lifted another flap. Then the man's face twisted in disgust and he dropped the bundle on the porch boards. Something that looked like a dead rat wrapped in dark gray feathers rolled toward Hoochie. Hoochie whimpered, struggled up, and sniffed it.

"A dead eaglet," Rocky pronounced, directing a glare that Peter had never seen on him toward his sister. "No thanks, we have supper planned already."

"You think it's a joke?" Skye's voice rose as her eyes did a quick diversion to the hammock. "It's not enough that you're disturbing our peace and pumping smelly fuel into our lake. Not enough that you're driving people away from our commune. You have to kill eagle chicks before they've even had a chance to fly out of the nest?"

"Who's killing eaglets?" Rocky's voice boomed. "Where do you get off accusing people of such ridiculous things? You've seen eagle chicks die before. I've seen 'em die before. We both grew up here, or have you forgotten that? It's survival of the fittest, Skye. Some live, some die. No one's killing your precious eagles, least of all me."

Skye's face went from pale to red to crimson all in one heart pump. "Rocky, we've been keeping watch on this lake's eagles for ten years. Counting them, recording them, tracking them. While you've been off playing. This"—her face contorted into grief as she gazed at the small feathered body that her brother had dropped—"is the third one this week. The third."

She waited. Rocky said nothing, just stood tall. Karma sprang out of the hammock to scoop up the eaglet's limp body and cradle it in its cloth against her chest.

"That's more than double what was going on before you came back here, Rocky. And nothing's different this year except you and your wakeboarding school." Skye's final words came out like a volume of spit. Hoochie, who'd sunk back down on the porch, lifted his head and looked from brother to sister, as if waiting for a cue from his master.

Rocky took a long, deep breath. He clenched and unclenched his fists. "Skye, calm down. I know the eagles are important to you. To your community. But this isn't really about the eagles, is it?"

Peter, who'd pressed himself tightly into his chair, stole a look at Jake. His buddy was jerking his head toward the cabin's open door. Right. Time to disappear. Leave these two alone to duke it out. Poor Karma. But she had to decide for herself where she wanted to be.

Peter rose and all but tiptoed behind Rocky, whose hands were now on his hips, his face flushed. Peter followed Jake indoors and shot a quick, backward glance at the hammock. Karma hadn't moved. He shut the door quietly.

Unfortunately, Rocky's voice carried right in through the living room window, clear and strong. "You come up with some excuse to try and shut me down just as I'm starting to make a living. You can't handle that I'm back, and that I might make a success of myself, can you? That wouldn't jive with ten years of calling me a bum. You can't handle that I might be working and doing what I love? And living where I want, whether you want me to or not."

He hadn't even finished the last sentence when Peter felt the cabin shake with a stomp from one of Skye's bare feet. Next, the window glass seemed to tremble with her screaming stream of words.

"Mom and Dad . . . lazy, irresponsible . . . dead fish . . . eagle sanctuary . . ."

Then came Rocky's voice, finally having lost patience: "Hippie crap . . . Nothing to do with my dog or boats . . . !"

Peter put his hands over his ears. Jake slumped into a chair and did the same. The door opened a crack. Karma slipped in and shut it softly behind her. Tears were spilling down her cheeks as she fled to her bedroom and closed the door, the eaglet bundle still in one hand.

Peter leaned back just far enough to look out the

window. He glimpsed Forrest standing as still as a tree that had taken root on the beach. His back was turned; he was staring out over the lake that divided the family he was daring to marry into.

"What do you think?" Peter whispered to Jake.

Jake was frowning. "I think . . . we should put on Rocky's headphones and listen to some heavy metal."

"Right." As Peter scouted around for headphones, he heard Skye's feet flying down the front steps. Rocky's voice called after her, "Get yourself an eagle specialist to do some tests, Skye. Then you'll know, okay? Then we'll both know . . ."

That's when Peter glimpsed Forrest swing around on the beach and step forward. "Don't listen to him, Skye. That would cost a fortune. We don't have that kind of money."

"You—stay—out—of—this!" Rocky roared.

That prompted Hoochie to growl.

Peter clamped the headphones on and cranked up the volume of a song he didn't even like. It was nearly loud enough to drown out the sound of Hoochie barking.

Not much of a bark, Peter thought. Then again, Hoochie's a lovable retriever, not a fierce guard dog. He was bred to chase birds, jump for Frisbees, and play first mate to the rockingest wakeboard school founder in the Northwest. A livelihood the dog seemed to sense was threatened.

11   Ocean Swells

"Jake, Peter! Wake up!" Rocky was shaking Jake by the shoulders.

Jake opened his eyes, smelled the dusty air of the barn. He tried to orient himself. Light streamed through the barn window. But it felt too early to get up. Besides, it was Sunday. Their first day off. No kids today.

"What?" he asked, rising and bumping his head on the underside of Peter's bunk.

"Huh?" Peter moaned from up above. "Rocky? What gives?"

"It's our day to go into Bellingham, remember? Wakeboard on the ocean?"

Jake checked his watch. "It's only seven, Rocky. Give us another hour of shut-eye, huh?"

Rocky sighed and sat down on the edge of Jake's bed. "We gotta go early. I want to stop at the pet emergency hospital on the way. Want them to have a quick look at Hoochie."

"Hoochie?" Jake was wide awake now. "Something wrong with Hoochie?"

"Not sure. He's hardly eaten for two days. And he seems unsteady on his feet. Probably no big deal, but since we're going into town, I phoned. They said they could take a look if we come in early."

Jake nodded. If he'd learned anything at all about Rocky since they'd met him on Lake Powell, it was that Hoochie was the most important thing in Rocky's life. His dog was more important to him, Jake would bet, than even the wakeboard school. He loved Hoochie the way Skye loved eagles. Hoochie was his family.

"Sure." Jake sprang out of bed and pulled his clothing on as Peter half fell out of the top bunk to do the same.

After a rushed breakfast, Jake, Peter, and Karma helped Rocky load the van.

"It's windy," Peter observed. "Maybe we'll get lucky and find some waves to surf. Ever surfed?" Peter was asking Karma as they pulled the van doors shut and Rocky turned the key in the ignition.

"No!" she said. "But you guys have surfed really big stuff, right? Jake told me about a thirty-foot wave during a storm?"

Jake chuckled as his mind flashed back to a hair-raising adventure he and Peter had survived well north of where they were. "Not on purpose," he reminded her. "But we've sure never wakeboarded in surf with a Jet Ski towing us. It'd be awesome if there were real waves today!"

"Pretty rare near Bellingham, but it is windy and we can hope." Karma pulled Hoochie's head into her lap. She stroked his back until he opened one eye, then shut it again. Jake watched Hoochie's chest rise and fall more rapidly than normal. He looked tired, but nothing more.

Jake sat back and watched trees flash by. He spotted an eagle soaring slowly overhead. Its distinctive white head and tail feathers and its enormous wingspan mesmerized him. So graceful, so timeless. Here before man. Part of the Northwest's past, present—and future, hopefully.

"How're those eagle eggs doing?" Jake asked Karma, remembering the eagle-watching platform.

"Oh! I didn't tell you. One in that nest has hatched already. The other is ready to pip any time," she said, smiling.

"Pip?" Peter asked.

"The chick is about to peck its way out. That can take a whole day, or more."

"A whole day?" Jake was amazed.

"Yup. If they take much longer than that, the inside of the shell dries out, gets all sticky like super glue, and they get stuck in there and die."

"No way. Can't the mother or other chick help them out a little?"

Karma shook her head and stroked Hoochie again. "Nope. The others just watch; they never help. My mom says it's nature's way."

"That's kind of brutal," Peter spoke up.

"Yup, but I think the second eaglet will be okay."

"We second-borns are tougher than we look!" Rocky joked from the driver's seat.

An image flashed through Jake's mind of Skye, the older sibling, watching solemnly from her corner of the nest as Rocky's beak slowly tap-tap-tapped from inside the shell. It made Jake smile.

"Tell me something else about eagles," Jake urged Karma.

"They're very territorial. They don't like to nest within three miles of each other."

Or five, in Skye and Rocky's case, Jake thought.

"Can Jake and I come watch the second chick hatch?" Peter asked.

Karma's smile lit up her face. "Of course." Then she hesitated. "Except, our community doesn't have a phone for letting you know when it starts. Only Forrest does, a cell that doesn't work all that well up here anyway."

"Hmmm, guess you'll have to send smoke signals or bike over," Peter joked. "Anyway, if you can get us in time, it'd be fun to climb those ladders to the platform and watch the little guy poke his way out."

"I'll try," Karma promised.

"Hey Rocky, where are the tunes?" Peter said, leaning forward toward the driver's seat.

Yeah, tunes, Jake thought. He'd never driven with Rocky when anyone could hold much of a conversation over the music. Rocky hadn't even touched the radio button.

"Givin' Hoochie some quiet time," Rocky said as the first houses of Bellingham appeared. A frown tugged at his mouth.

At the animal hospital, a smiling receptionist greeted Hoochie and offered him a dish of water. Jake listened to Hoochie's slurping sounds as he lapped it up, then lifted his nose to sniff the room's air. Jake smelled medicines and disinfectant. He looked at people huddled in the waiting room, clutching kittens or sticking their fingers through holes in dog carriers to reassure barking canines. He wanted out of this place. He wanted onto a saltwater wave.

A vet with gray hair, a white lab coat, a kindly face, and a stethoscope around his neck ushered Hoochie and Rocky into an examination room.

The boys remained in the waiting room. "What's

going to be your best trick today?" Peter asked Jake.

Jake considered this. "I'm going to try for a tantrum off the lip of a wave. Should be easier on a moving wave than on the lake, I figure. What about you?"

"I'm gonna try a roll to blind," Peter said, sticking his feet up on a coffee table.

"Remember to keep your eyes closed more here, 'cause saltwater stings," Karma warned him.

Rocky walked back into the reception room just then, shoulders drooped, worry lines showing above his bandanna.

"What'd they say, Uncle Rocky? Where's Hoochie?"

"They want to do some tests on him. Take X-rays. Want to keep him till two o'clock. Said I can't stay with him," Rocky said, removing his bandanna and mopping his brow with it.

"Oh." Karma wrapped an arm around her uncle's shoulders. "Well, if he needs tests, he's in a good place. You did the right thing dropping him off."

"And the Jet Skiing will be a perfect distraction. We'll finish up before two and be back in time to hear what they say," Peter added.

"Okay," Rocky said in a husky voice. He ushered the boys toward the examination room and opened the door a crack. Hoochie lay on his side atop a metal table on wheels. A pool of black vomit puddled beside his head.

"Hoochie!" Rocky cried in distress.

"Eeew," Jake said, grossed out. "Poor Hoochie. He really isn't feeling well."

A young female attendant smiled sympathetically at the little group. She looked ready to wheel the dog out through a far door. Rocky stepped further into the room and leaned over his dog until Hoochie lifted his nose. "You'll be okay. They'll take good care of you. Be good, boy. Love ya."

"Me too," Karma said quietly.

"And me," Peter said, fingers pinching his nose as he stared at Hoochie's vomit.

Jake reached to pat the retriever's soft coat. "See you at two," he said as cheerfully as he could. The four watched as the attendant nodded and pushed the table through a door marked "Staff Only."

"Hey, Rocky," Peter said as they emerged outside. "Can Jake and I take a turn on the Jet Ski while you wakeboard?"

Rocky glanced at the Jet Ski on his trailer as if noticing it for the first time that morning. He glanced back at the vet hospital. "Nope. Wouldn't be responsible of me."

Jake was dumbstruck. Rocky had been letting them operate the Jet Skis and Hoochie's Ride for more than a week. Of course, that was up at the lake. Jet Skiing in the wind on the ocean would be more dangerous. Still, it wasn't like Rocky. Oh well. All the more action on wakeboards, Jake figured.

Rocky drove right onto the beach, to where the foam of spent waves raced onto dry sand.

"We're in luck," he ruled. "There's surf!" Under the screech of seagulls and beside the crash of the gentle, glassy rollers, Rocky and the youths unloaded the Jet Ski, changed into wetsuits, and readied their boards.

"It's so early, we have the beach to ourselves," Peter observed.

"And the surf's perfect," Jake nodded, his toes squelching in the wet sand as he hopped about, pulling on a wetsuit boot. "The wind's calmed down and the wave sets are breaking just right for a session."

"I'm just gonna watch," Karma volunteered. She hauled a camping chair out of the van, plunked it down on the beach, and produced a camera. "Do me some real action out there."

"Just make sure you watch out for the undertow," Rocky warned them, eyes squinting at sparkling waves. "I'm gonna be pulling you into the surf. You can either let go of the rope when you're on the wave, or let me pull you into the sweet spot and do tricks off the lip."

Rocky pushed the Jet Ski into the surf. He tied the tow rope to the back of the machine and threw the handle to Jake.

"I'm stoked!" Jake said, nodding as Rocky powered into the surf. Seconds later, Jake tasted salt and squeezed the sting from his eyes as he plowed up and through the foamy wash around the break. His heart pumped as he gripped the tow-rope handle and headed out to sea. Turning his head briefly to take in Peter and Karma on the beach, he almost missed Rocky's shout as the man pointed to the horizon.

"There's a great set coming right at you!"

Jake turned, smiled, and tightened his hold on the handle. Rocky pulled him right into the sweet spot; Jake exploded down the face of a head-high, glassy roller. As the rope tightened, Jake loaded the line and edged up and off the top of the wave, throwing a huge roll to blind. Wild cheering sounded from the beach. He threw the handle and surfed the wave until it closed on him. The white wash's embrace felt friendly. "Alright!"

Bobbing up and down, he waved his hand to direct Rocky his way. Hope he picks me up before another wave comes and pounds both of us, he thought. His adrenalin surged with an oncoming wave as Rocky zipped around and grabbed his outstretched hand. Rocky's strong yank lifted Jake onto the back of the ski just in time. As Rocky squeezed the throttle, the two burst out of the way of a head-high wave. Go, go, go Jake urged the machine silently. He breathed easier as it propelled the two of them right up onto the wet sand of the beach.

"That was incredible!" Karma proclaimed, running toward them.

"Nice roll to revert," Peter said, lifting his arms lazily in a stretch.

They played for hours, then took a break in town for lunch. Rocky treated them to submarine sandwiches. Jake and Peter gobbled down foot-long ones packed with meat while Karma, eyeing the boys with a smile, said she was very happy with her six-inch veggie sub.

Back in the water after sunning themselves for a while, Peter addressed Jake, "Okay, ready? Watch this."

"Go for it," Jake said with a grin. He watched Peter strap on his bindings and hop over to grab the handle.

"Watch out for the undertow," Jake reminded him. "It's strong."

"No worries," Peter replied. He slung his powerful legs over the back of the waiting Jet Ski.

"Have fun!" Karma called, waving as Rocky pulled Peter out into the whitecapped surf.

Jake and Karma shaded their eyes to follow the pair past where the waves were breaking.

"Peter's climbing onto the back of the Jet Ski," Karma observed.

Then, mysteriously, the wave sets paused.

"Rocky's stopped," Jake commented.

"Mother Nature isn't cooperating," Karma suggested.

"Nah," Jake said. "The ocean's just waiting to surprise them with a big one!"

Hardly were the words out of his mouth when he spotted a set over the horizon. Jake watched Peter swivel his head seaward. Rocky fired up the Jet Ski and pulled the line tight.

"Wait for it!" Jake mumbled, tensing.

"Rocky's towing him into position!" Karma announced, leaping about. "It's a way big one, Jake! Isn't that more dangerous?"

"Yeah, like a ten-footer," Jake mumbled in awe, a little jealous. "But he'll ace it." He watched Rocky tow Peter right into the sweet spot and Peter launch down the face of the monster. He felt his own pulse pick up as Peter started getting comfortable on the wave.

"Yes!" Jake and Karma cheered together as Peter popped off the top and struck a sweet heelside-frontside 540, then a switch-indy tantrum.

"He's totally dominating the surf!" Jake enthused.

"Here they come!" Karma added, clapping her hands together as Rocky pulled Peter back toward shore. Jake watched, the pounding waves keeping time with his heartbeats. "You'd think he'd been doing this for years," Karma said, leaning forward and clasping her hands together.

"Not bad," Jake agreed, grinning. He was too pleased for his buddy to be truly jealous. But as he eyed the waves behind Peter, he also knew their session was over.

"Waves are getting way too big. Undertow's getting stronger," Rocky shouted as he dismounted the Jet Ski and let Jake and Karma help him pull it farther up the beach.

"No place for the timid. That second wave was really scary," Peter asserted to no one in particular.

"No kidding," Rocky confirmed, his eyes locked on a new wave set. "Could drown you if you weren't paying attention. Anyway, we should get back to Hoochie."

"Okay by me," Jake ruled, a little relieved.

"He'd have loved watching us," Peter said.

"Got that right," Rocky said, nodding sadly. "Pack it up, kids."

At two o'clock sharp, they pulled up at the animal hospital. The receptionist seemed to remember Rocky; she led him straight into an examination room. Karma followed at his heels, not waiting for permission. Jake and Peter trailed in last. Hoochie belonged to all of them, Jake thought, and if he was sick, he'd be pleased to see all of them.

The gray-haired vet stood alone in the room. His lab coat looked more disheveled than earlier, and he wore no stethoscope. His sober eyes took in the circle of people.

Jake rested a hand on the cold stainless steel of the examination table.

"We lost Hoochie an hour ago," the vet said, his eyes meeting each of theirs, then resting on the table.

"Lost him?" Rocky's voice came out choked. His face twisted into something painful to look at. His big hands shot out for the examination table.

Jake tried desperately to picture Hoochie escaping out the hospital's back door, sniffing the fresh, salt-filled air, and sprinting happily for the beach. He could picture Hoochie's big ears flapping, tail wagging, nose pointed confidently toward where his master was plying the surf.

The vet rested an arm on Rocky's shoulder as Karma moved to bury her face in Rocky's chest.

Jake felt his heart slow to a stop. He looked at Peter's stricken face.

"The X-ray showed an enlarged liver and bleeding ulcers," the vet continued, each word measured and painstakingly delivered. "We think it's a case of poison."

12   The Pipping

Jake approached the two mounds behind Rocky's cabin slowly, a watering can in his hand. He peered past Peter's hunched form at the bright flowers atop each mound. He used his fingers to poke them down a little further into the dirt. Then, as the pungent perfume of the poppies and daisies rose to his nostrils, he watered them.

Finally, he sat down heavily on the ground and sighed. One mound was small, small enough for an eaglet. The eaglet Skye had brought Rocky, and which Karma had decided needed a formal burial. The mound beside it was large, large enough for the biggest-hearted golden retriever Jake had ever known. The dog's chewed Frisbee served as a grave marker. Both mounds were all too fresh.

"Karma's flowers look nice," Peter said, his voice a monotone.

"They're organic, from her garden," Jake said, not that it had anything to do with anything. It was just something to say. The forest seemed quiet today, as if grieving Hoochie in its own way. Even the squirrels Hoochie had chased, the birds he'd barked at, appeared to be holding a moment of respectful silence.

"Rocky's taking it pretty hard, huh?" Peter's voice remained flat. "He hasn't been himself at all."

Jake thought about how there'd been no music, no laughter, no jumping off roofs, not even a "rockingest wakeboard school" greeting when the kids arrived. Nor had Rocky shown any interest, during the two days since Hoochie had died, in wakeboarding with his junior instructors after hours. Strangely, too, he'd refused to touch the Jet Skis in the boathouse, operating only Hoochie's Ride.

"The kids have been taking it hard, too," Jake said, lying on his back and staring way up at the eagle's heavy woven-stick nest above the graves. "Especially Dougie. Even the new kids seem to have heard about Hoochie."

"Yeah." Peter picked up some stones and began tossing them into the forest. "Rocky's taking his time coming back from town. It's almost suppertime, and we need groceries."

They did need groceries, Jake knew. The cupboards were almost bare, even though Rocky had hardly eaten a thing the last two nights. In fact, it had been up to Jake and Peter to make their own dinners lately. And Jake, for one, was getting tired of Rocky's junk food. The stuff Rocky had stocked made him crave Tao's cheese-cauliflower casserole.

"Pretty boring without Karma around," Peter groused, hurling a small gray stone against a tree. "I bought a new computer game in Bellingham for her, and she hasn't even been over to try it."

Jake nodded. No Karma, no Hoochie, and a Rocky who seemed to be a shadow of his usual self. It was boring around here, except during the kids' lessons. But Karma had made a deal with her mom and Forrest: no more skipping out of community "activities." That meant the only time they'd see her now was weekends. Today was only Tuesday.

"Jake! Peter!" came a faraway voice up the trail that stretched around Eagle Lake.

"Karma?" Jake shaded his eyes and poked Peter in the ribs. "Is that Karma? I was just thinking about how we wouldn't see her until the weekend."

They stood and rushed to where the path came into the cabin's clearing. From the other direction, Karma was tearing toward them on her bike like someone bent on winning the Tour de France.

"It's pipping!" she shouted. "Want to come see? It's pipping!"

Jake and Peter looked at each other, then glanced at the empty cabin. "I'll write Rocky a note," Jake volunteered.

"Can we take a Jet Ski back?" Karma asked, her words coming in gasps. "It'll be faster to start up than Hoochie's Ride."

Jake was considering this, wondering what Rocky would say, when Peter spoke up.

"Good idea, Karma! Rocky won't mind!"

The two of them hauled the craft out of the boathouse and were readying it at lake's edge when Jake emerged from the cabin, still thinking it wasn't a good idea.

"I'm driving," Karma declared with a glint in her eyes.

They're not going to listen to me anyway, Jake thought. He climbed on behind Karma. Peter climbed on behind Jake.

"Hold on tight!" she shouted.

The girl meant tight. Jake's knees gripped the Jet Ski and his hands clung for dear life to Karma's waist as the machine burst into action. He couldn't imagine how Peter was managing to stay aboard behind him. The Jet Ski wasn't really designed to hold three, and if Karma wasn't so small, Peter would have spilled off the back end on the first lurch.

"Karma! Slow down!" Jake shouted in her ear,

hardly believing he would ask such a thing. But she was nuts, a bucking bronco loosed into a ring. She seemed to take delight in veering left and right just for the thrill of it. Jake, mouth ajar and knuckles white, looked in terror at the oncoming rail and slider, fervently hoping she wasn't going to try jumping or grinding either with two riders on back.

He breathed a little easier after she passed them. But as she circled back abruptly to catch a little air over the machine's own wake, he swallowed hard and ducked his head behind her. What was she on, anyway? Maybe she'd eaten a fermented zucchini or something.

Luckily, the lake was only about five miles long, and at fifty miles an hour, even with a few wild-woman switchbacks, they were soon approaching the commune's waterfront.

As she cut the motor, Jake turned to look at Peter.

"Sweet ride," Peter enthused, trying to high-five Jake. "I told you she has a wild streak in her." He sounded proud, like a dad bragging about his kid. Jake was speechless.

"Perfect!" Karma said, running her played-out bronco up on shore. "Way faster than a bike, any day!"

Jake wasn't sure what to make of the way her lips twisted into a tight, satisfied smile at the sight of Forrest's frame suddenly filling the doorway of the yellow lodge. His expression, Jake reflected, was darker than thunderclouds.

"Come on!" Karma urged Jake and Peter as she slipped into one of the safety harnesses at the bottom of the tree and clipped its carabiner to the safety rope. "Up the ladder before that chick's out of his egg!"

They stepped into harnesses and scurried up after her without a backward glance at Forrest or the other commune members who had emerged to stand and gape at the Jet Ski. It had been a pretty deafening arrival, Jake admitted. Should he have refused Karma's request to bring it over? He'd only been thinking of what Rocky would say, not Karma's community. Oh well, he had to concentrate on his footing right now and moving his safety carabiner steadily upwards.

"How high is that platform?" Peter asked, breathing hard ahead of Jake.

"A hundred and twenty feet. That's like twelve storeys," she said, hands and feet working the series of rope ladders as if she climbed them every day. Which she actually did, Jake realized. "Our telescope has to be as high as the tree that holds the nest. Eagles always choose one of the tallest trees so ravens and gulls and squirrels don't try to eat their eggs. Also to keep away from mosquitoes," she said, swatting at one on her cheek.

"And to see fish in the lake," Jake suggested.

"Yup."

As if on cue, one of the eagles left the nest across the clearing and whooshed down past them, wings lifted to a V. Then it dropped sharply toward the lake, which was already looking like a puddle from their height. Sweeping in a slow circle, it locked its wings and brought its wicked-looking talons to the front, exposing its white tail feathers like bloomers beneath a windblown skirt. The giant yellow talons skidded across the water surface like a plane's touchdown, but just as quickly rose, a salmon clenched in those claws. More slowly now, the eagle rose, higher and higher, until it landed on the edge of the massive bowl of sticks that served as its nest.

"The dad's brought them supper," Karma proclaimed. Seconds later, she neared the platform and Jake looked up to see Tao lean down to give her a hand up.

"Hey, Tao. Thanks for taking the end of my shift. I've brought visitors."

"So I see," Tao said, running his fingers through his Afro and smiling at Jake and Peter as their heads appeared, one by one. He offered each a hand up and directed them to the telescope.

"Whoa," Jake said. "There really is one chick and one egg in that nest." He couldn't believe how fluffy and gray the hatched chick was.

Karma giggled. "Told you. And soon there'll be two chicks. Is the mom helping the dad tear that salmon up into bite-sized pieces?"

"Yeah. If that's the mom."

"Lemme see!" Peter protested.

"The mom's the larger one," Karma informed them. "The dad flies in and out more, but they both do babysitting."

"I can see the beak of the pipping one! I can see the eye! That eggshell's gonna fall apart in a second!" Peter enthused.

"My turn!" Jake insisted. "Cool. Get a load of that tiny hooked beak. It has a big knob on it. He's really hammering on that thing from inside."

"I want to see!" Peter said, grabbing the telescope away from Jake. "Hey, that's mean! The older chick just took a swipe at the hatching chick."

"They always do," Tao's voice informed them casually. "The older chick, especially if it's a female, always dominates and bullies. Sometimes even kills her sibling. But they call a truce if they both make it to three weeks."

Jake shook his head in amazement, then dared to look sideways at Karma. "So your mom and uncle haven't made it to three weeks yet."

He heard a low chuckle from Tao.

Karma looked at Jake with a startled expression,

then allowed a slow smile and a glance down the tree. "Uh-oh. Here she comes now."

Jake and Peter continued to take turns watching, with occasional commentary from Tao or Karma, for the next ten minutes. But Jake noticed that Karma went quiet as the sounds of someone's feet scuffing against bark began nearing the platform.

When Skye's blonde head and pained face appeared, the only sound was an eagle's screech across the clearing.

"Karma, you're to come down this instant."

"But Mom, they wanted to see the second chick pip. I promised I'd tell them and we don't have a phone. How else was I going to . . ."

"You left your eagle shift early to do it."

"Tao said it'd be okay."

"You didn't ask me permission. And you came back on that noisy, polluting thing"—she waved her hand to the lake below, where the Jet Ski sat, looking as small as a mosquito.

Karma threw a helpless look at Jake and Peter. Jake sat frozen to the platform, hand on a railing as if guarding against being pushed off, even though, of course, his safety rope was still on.

"You boys can stay a while longer as long as you're here," Skye said, eyes resting on Tao after a quick sweep over Jake and Peter. "It's good for you to see what my brother seems set on poisoning."

Jake opened his mouth but found no words in it. Anyway, the stern head had disappeared again, and Karma had already checked her safety line and swung a leg onto the ladder's first rung.

"See you later," she said, her voice hoarse.

Jake heard Tao sigh, and he turned to see Peter's eyebrows knit into one long one.

Then, "He's out!" Tao's voice sounded. "And dodging his sister's beak very nicely, I'd say."

For the next half hour, like the squabbling hatchlings they were watching, Jake, Peter, and Tao jockeyed for time on the telescope.

13 Accusations

"It's your fault, Peter." Jake, feet hanging over the dock back at the cabin the next morning, was kicking the air furiously. His ears were still ringing with the angry torrent of words inside the yellow lodge as the boys had all but tiptoed past to head home on the Jet Ski. "Karma's probably going to be grounded for weeks. You've encouraged her to do stuff that gets her into trouble ever since we met her. Why? You've seen what her parents are like."

"Parents? Forrest isn't her dad. Anyway, he has no right to push people around like he does. No wonder two more people left the commune this week. It's all falling apart 'cause he's too strict. Karma said so herself."

"That's none of your business, Peter. And Forrest is going to be her stepdad soon whether she likes it or not. Whether you like it or not. We shouldn't have taken the Jet Ski over to the commune."

"It was her idea."

"And you jumped all over it. You encouraged her. You're totally into getting her in trouble, Peter. Admit it."

"I'm into seeing her enjoy life a little. That place is like a prison. I feel sorry for her."

"Yeah? What about Rocky? You think getting Karma to play video games and eat chocolate bars is helping things with him and Skye? Next you'll be getting her to eat meat."

"Skye's a grump. Can't blame Rocky for not liking her."

Jake balled his hands into fists and stared at the water. Maybe he should jump in to cool off. Peter sure wasn't listening to him. Instead, Jake jerked his head up as he heard the sound of Rocky's van approaching.

"Kids are here. Lighten up, old buddy," Peter said, jumping up.

Peter's words only made a pulse in Jake's forehead thump harder. Then he saw Dougie's smiling face hanging out the window of the front seat and the boy's arms waving like crazy.

"Jake!" Dougie shouted happily.

Jake forced a smile onto his face, rose, and started lining up the life jackets. Let's see, Dougie had mastered a 180 last time. Maybe he'd manage a 360 today with some special encouragement. Jake took a deep breath of the fresh air and surrounding Douglas firs and yanked his sunglasses from where they sat in his thick brown hair. He willed his frustration with Peter to subside.

"Dougie, dude," he greeted his favorite student. "How's it going?"

"Okay," Dougie said, eyes darting about the beach. "Where's Karma?"

"Uh, she's not teaching today. She's busy."

Dougie's smile evaporated and he turned accusing eyes on Jake. He lifted one of his little feet and stomped it on the beach. "I want you and Karma for teachers today. Where's Karma?"

Hmmm, Jake thought. So much for my Mr. Cool-Guy Instructor act.

"Karma is across the lake. She's, um, looking after a new eagle baby. Come on, let's get started on teaching you a 360."

Dougie pointed a stubby finger at Jake as if it were a lie detector blinking red. "Is the eagle baby sick? Poisoned like Hoochie?"

Jake's jaw loosened, and he looked about to make sure no one else had heard that. Luckily, no one was in earshot. "Dougie! Who said anything about Hoochie being poisoned? And no, this eagle baby isn't sick."

Dougie drew himself up as tall as his four-foot-something body would let him. "My granddad's a vet," he declared. "He was there when Hoochie died. He thinks this lake might be poisoned."

Jake knelt down so that he was face to face with this brash brat. "Dougie, this lake is not poisoned, and if I hear you say that one more time, I will have Rocky drive you right home. Do you understand?"

The kid shrank half an inch and stared at the dirt between his toes before nodding.

"So, you're up for a 360 today?"

"Okay." But he'd turned his head to stare at Hoochie's grave.

"Jake?"

"Yes, Dougie." Jake braced himself, not knowing what to expect next.

"What's your best trick?"

"A tantrum to blind."

Dougie's eyes lit up, and one of the students who'd moved toward them shouted, "Hey, everyone, Jake can do a tantrum to blind! Show us, Jake! Show us!"

"Hey, I'm here to teach you guys, not show off."

"Oh, show 'em, Jake," Rocky teased.

"Go for it, old buddy," Peter joined in. "Then I'll do 'em a whirlybird and Rocky can do 'em a hoochie."

Everyone's face froze for a second, Peter's included, at the mention of the deceased dog's name. But Rocky nodded, as if he'd been waiting for the suggestion. "Yes, he'd like that. It would be the right thing to do.

I'll pay my respects by doing a hoochie."

Jake had been trying tantrum to blinds for a while. He'd almost perfected them. Still, landing "blind" or away from the boat with the handle behind your back was pretty tricky. With the kids egging him on, he set up behind Rocky on Hoochie's Ride. Soon he was up and moving, carefully squaring up his shoulders.

He went for a smooth, rounded turn toward the wake on his heelside. "Don't load the line," he reminded himself. "Focus on speed."

Speed was what it was all about. Speed, and landing it right. Especially in front of all his students. What would they think if he blew it?

No pressure, he kidded himself. At the top of the wake, he dug the toes of his feet in with all he had. He turned his shoulders, released his trailing hand, pushed off, and arched his back. Yes! He felt the thrill of being up in the air, heading for upside-down, board drawing a neat arc in the clear blue sky.

It was a fully laid-out backflip, but he wasn't done yet. Coming out of his rotation, he spotted his landing with all the alertness of an eagle hunting fish. Now he took his lead hand, turned clockwise away from the boat, and gripping the handle, moved it to the base of his spine. Like he was hiding a surprise from Dougie behind his back. The landing sent up a victorious rooster tail of spray. It also inspired an approving roar from the high-pitched audience on shore. Jake grinned a relaxed grin, tossed the handle away like a Frisbee, and sank slowly and happily.

"Peter! Peter! Peter!" the audience changed its cheer as Rocky headed back to his next customer. Jake watched Peter raise his arms to his fans, playing his moment for all he was worth.

Once hooked up, he rose like a star and approached the wake just as Jake had, as if preparing for a regular heelside tantrum. Up, up he flew, to oohs and ahs from the beach. The instant he was upside-down, he took the handle in his lead hand and pulled it across his face. Like a toy whose string had been pulled, he went into a twirling motion—rotating like helicopter blades until his lead foot came forward and glided his board to a smooth landing.

Clapping, hooting, and hollering rose from shore, sending some ducks flying overhead into noisy quacking as they disappeared over the trees.

"Nice," Jake complimented Peter as his friend stepped onto shore.

"Not so bad yourself," his friend returned, shaking his wet blond curls till Jake had to shield his face from the onslaught of droplets.

"Now it's Rocky's hoochie time. I'll drive the boat. You spot," Peter suggested.

"Okay by me," Jake agreed. "Do us proud," he

instructed Rocky, giving him a high-five as he climbed into the boat.

"Best I can for an old-school guy," Rocky teased back.

Jake found his hands clenching his seat as Peter pulled the boat into position. A hoochie glide, he knew, was a dangerous, advanced trick. Sure it was a thrill to leap up and extend your board-latched feet out behind you, flying like Superman. Still, Jake's stomach knotted just thinking about the big risk factor. Hitting the water face-first at twenty-plus miles an hour was a good way to snuff yourself out. Jake knew he was close to having the skill; he just needed to have the guts to try it one of these days. Of course, Rocky had years of wakeboarding on both the boys, and a fluid confidence that was a treat to watch. And he'd done hoochies lots of times before, Jake reminded himself.

Even so, as Jake watched Rocky's muscled legs push him off the top of the wake, he felt his teeth start to grind. Moving close to twenty miles an hour, Rocky pulled his arm and shoulder forward over his toes until he was flying head first. As if that wasn't impressive enough, he then reached back with gloved fingers to pinch the edge of his board, all while face-forward. At the climax of the move, he arched his powerful back, grinning for show. He made for an impressive Superman, if Superman flew with a colorful, sticker-covered board on his feet, minus a cape and gripping a bar. Then, as Jake held his breath, the smooth-boarding owner of the Wakeup Wakeboard School brought his knees up, pulled the handle in, and landed safely on his heels, rear end crouched over the water till he let the rope draw him up.

He'd done his dog proud, Jake thought, clapping as he let his gaze wander to Hoochie's grave.

When he swiveled his head to speak to Peter, how-ever, he caught sight of a bicyclist bumping along the lakeside trail into their clearing.

Judging from Rocky's slumped shoulders and slow trudge up to the beach, he'd seen his sister, too.

"Guess we'd better dock," Peter said with a sigh.

"Mmm," Jake agreed.

Within minutes, Rocky and his junior instructors were standing together solemnly watching her final approach. They were all but oblivious to the jumping kids gathered around them, trying to congratulate them.

"Skye." Rocky looked at her with a slightly pained expression. "I hear the second chick hatched. Jake and Peter really enjoyed watching it. They came back with lots of questions about eagles."

"Did they?" Skye's face looked kind of puffy to Jake. He detected dark circles under her eyes, as if she hadn't slept all night. "Could you answer any of their questions, Rocky?" She ignored the children, who had quieted down and were staring at her.

The question was a challenge, the sarcasm was there, but her voice was weary and weak, as if she didn't really have the heart for a fight.

Rocky seemed to detect the change in her. "Actually," he said more softly, "yes. Reminded me of when you and I used to watch them. You taught me enough to answer all their questions." His eyes were on hers, perhaps looking for a sign of truce.

Her eyes moved to the graves and she was silent for a minute. "Sorry about your dog," she finally said. "What's in the second grave?"

"The eaglet you brought over."

Surprise passed over her face like a veil, then it was gone. She heaved a sigh and stood there, looking fragile enough to fall over.

"Are you a wakeboarder?" Dougie piped up, but Skye didn't seem to hear him.

"Skye, are you okay?" Rocky asked, taking a step toward her.

"No," she said so quietly that Jake could barely hear her. "Karma's been missing since early this morning. Is she here? Have you seen her?"

Rocky shook his head. "No, Skye, she hasn't been around." His sigh was audible. He shook his head again, face clouding with concern and sympathy.

Jake noticed that the kids had gone very quiet.

Now Skye turned to Jake and Peter, her eyes pleading. "Have you? Would you tell me if she were here? Please?"

"She hasn't been over here," Jake said, voice steady and eyes meeting hers, which looked ready to spill tears. "We'll look out for her."

"Are you Karma's mom? We like Karma," one of the kids said.

Skye nodded vaguely, and her eyes returned to Rocky. "She and Forrest had a big fight. Then Forrest and I had a fight. If you see her, tell her Forrest has gone into Bellingham for a couple of days. Maybe she'll come home if she knows that."

"We'll tell her, Skye," Rocky said, moving a little closer to his sister and lifting a hand as if preparing to rest it on her bony shoulders. But Skye stepped back, twirled around, and began moving toward the path, weaving through the pack of children as if they were invisible. She halted in front of Karma's bike, the one the girl had left the previous afternoon when she'd hopped on the Jet Ski with the boys. Jake saw her shoulders tremble and her chin drop. Then she climbed onto her own bike and pedaled back toward the commune, slowly, listlessly, as if the trip over had drained her of all her energy.

14   River Ride

Peter was still wide awake just before midnight, lying with his hands behind his head in his top bunk. He could tell from Jake's breathing that his buddy was fast asleep below. Peter wished he could sleep, too. It had been a long day, teaching the kids, including doing that whirlybird for them—though he'd done it beautifully, if he did say so himself. And then there'd been the search for Karma once Rocky had returned from dropping the kids off. Rocky, Jake, and Peter had gone looking along the paths beside the lake and behind Rocky's cabin. They'd run into some folks from the commune doing the same. They'd all looked pretty haggard, like they'd been looking all day.

Peter had suggested to Rocky that they try up at the sawmill, but Rocky had said no, that would be trespassing. Jake and Peter hadn't dared to say that they'd been there the week before, shown the way by Karma.

It didn't sit easy with Peter that Jake was mad at him, would hardly look at him over their late dinner of microwaved corn dogs. It wasn't fair. It wasn't Peter's fault that Karma had run away. Jake didn't seem to get that Karma was doing bolder things and being a little rebellious because, well, because she was fifteen. Sure, Peter had played her along a little. But the girl needed encouragement to stand up to those over-strict rules over there, and to Forrest's dictator personality.

Okay, so Peter had been quick to get her into wakeboarding and had gotten a kick out of her taking the Jet Ski over to the commune. But there's no way it was Peter's fault that Karma, her mom, and Forrest had quarreled. She'd probably run because Forrest had yelled at her too much. Peter had wanted to cover his ears when he'd heard Forrest shouting at her the afternoon of the eaglet pipping. Had he grounded her for coming to let the boys know? So stupid to punish her for that. Eagles don't hatch every day, and you'd think the leader of an eagle-crazy commune would want the kids from across the lake to take an interest.

Anyway, even Skye had admitted this afternoon to Rocky that she'd had a fight with Forrest. Maybe that meant Karma's mom was learning to stand up to the ogre, too.

Of course, Peter was worried about Karma. Running away from home is kind of serious. As in, no food or place to stay. Then again, Karma knew which berries to pick around here, and she had a blanket stashed in the bird blind. She was probably just hiding for a day to make a point. It'd all work out.

"Psst."

Peter sat up. Where'd that come from? A strange, breathy sound. Mice rustling around again? He shivered as he felt night air hit his face.

"Psst. Anyone awake in here?"

"Karma!" Peter wriggled out of his sleeping bag and jumped down lightly. It was pitch black, but he thought he saw her outline in the doorway. "Flick the light on," he whispered.

"No!" The shadow moved to block the light switch. "Peter, do you have some spare blankets in here? And do you have any food?" She was keeping her voice barely audible.

"No food," he whispered. "Otherwise we get mice. But we have an extra sleeping bag in here, and I could go get some food from the cabin. Are you okay?"

"Of course I'm okay," she responded, almost too quickly. "Just cold and hungry. You won't tell anyone I'm here, will you? Just for tonight? I could sleep behind that stack of lumber in your loft. I'll be gone by morning."

"Gone? Gone where, Karma?" Peter shot a look over at Jake's bunk as he heard his friend moan and turn over. But Jake didn't wake. Peter lowered his voice. "What are you going to do, Karma?"

"I don't know," she said, her voice sounding drained. He could hear her teeth chattering. He felt around for an extra sleeping bag Rocky had left them for cold nights and handed it to Karma, who was at the bottom of the loft's ladder now. It was a moonless night, or else clouds had obscured any natural light. He still couldn't see anything but a silhouette climb the ladder. He was pleased she was safe, and that she trusted them to help her. He wanted to talk to her, ask her where she'd been, why she'd left. But she sounded so exhausted he didn't have the heart to keep her up.

"Good night, Karma," he whispered as he pulled on a jacket, slipped into some shoes, and checked to make sure Jake was still asleep. "I'll be back in a few minutes with some food so you'll have something to eat in the morning."

"Thanks, Peter. Good night."

*

In the morning, Peter had to stand on his upper bunk to see a small huddle inside a sleeping bag still behind the planks. She was sound asleep, one arm around her pack, which was filled with the food Peter had spirited out of the cabin last night. He crooked his neck to look closer at a shadow on her face. Something in his gut went tight. It was no shadow. It was a bruise. Someone had punched her in the face. No wonder she was on the run! No wonder she hadn't let him switch the light on last night and had promised to be gone by morning. But he was glad she was sleeping in. She must be exhausted.

Peter clenched his teeth and shook his head. No way would he let Forrest get his hands on their friend. Did Skye know? Is that why she'd had a falling out with Forrest too? Jake would say it was none of their business and not to interfere. But Peter guessed that Jake had no idea Karma was up in the loft, and he might think differently if he saw the bruise.

Quietly, Peter kneeled on his bed and lowered his head to inspect the bunk below. Empty. Jake was up and out. Peter dressed as quietly as he'd ever dressed. He stepped out of the barn, yawned, and stretched his arms over his head, struggling to fully wake up. He spotted Jake bent over the Jet Ski, which was sitting just up from the water. Peter decided not to tell Jake about Karma immediately. Not till he'd had some breakfast to wake him up and help him think about what they should do.

"Morning. Where's Rocky?" he asked.

"Gone to the commune to help Skye plan a search for Karma."

"No kidding!" Peter was more stunned that Rocky and Skye would plan something together than he was worried about hiding a fugitive for a morning.

"Something wrong with the Jet Ski?"

"Nope. Just tuning it up," Jake responded.

Peter smiled. Jake, the son of a mechanic, loved nothing more than having a wrench in one hand and an owner's manual diagram of engine parts in the other.

"Had breakfast?"

"Yeah. Left some French toast for you."

"Awesome. Thanks." Peter whistled as he headed for the cabin.

He was searching for a fork in the drying rack by the sink when a movement out the kitchen window made him straighten up. He focused on the woods behind the barn. Was that something or someone moving from behind one tree to another?

Peter's fork clattered into the sink. He sprinted to the cabin's back door and opened it a crack. He waited, sweaty palm on the doorknob, heart thumping. A minute, two minutes ticked by. Maybe he'd been imagining things. But no, there it was again: a figure darting behind another tree, this one closer to the barn's rear door. Peter clenched his teeth. There was no mistaking the tall, powerful figure.

Peter flung the back door wide open and broke

into a loud rendition of a song by his favorite band, Retrofire, as he sauntered toward the barn.

As he neared the building, he picked up two sticks and did a real, live drumbeat on the barn's walls where the song featured a drum solo. "Jake, are you up yet?" he called out before opening the door. "You lazy old thing. Just 'cause it's Sunday morning doesn't mean you can sleep in . . ."

He stepped inside. "Oh, guess he's outside then," he continued in a ridiculously loud voice, pretending to talk to himself. Then, breaking into a whisper, "Karma, Forrest is behind the barn trying to sneak in here."

He heard her draw in her breath, but admired how not a bit of her showed from behind that pile of lumber. He started opening and slamming dresser drawers, while hearing Karma crawl out of her sleeping bag and stow it in her pack, which she shrugged into.

"I'll try to get rid of him," Peter whispered.

He heard the Jet Ski's motor rev, heard Jake cheer "Yes!" He stepped out the front door.

"Hey Jake, there you are! I need you a second."

Jake raised his head and nodded before walking up the shore.

What Peter hadn't counted on was Forrest walking boldly out from behind the barn just then and confronting the two boys.

"Karma in there?" he asked bluntly. "Her mother and I have been searching for her all night. We're worried. You're not hiding her here, are you?"

Jake looked a little surprised, but collected himself quickly. "We've been searching for her too," he replied. "She hasn't been around here, not yet anyway. We were going to spend today looking."

"Have no idea where she is, but hope we find her today," Peter lied. Forrest stared at each in turn, then swung around and took long strides back into the woods.

"Not very friendly this morning, is he?" Jake commented.

"Is he ever?" Peter mumbled.

"Well, I have to get a tool from the cabin," Jake said and wandered off before Peter could decide how to tell him about Karma.

Peter waited a long time in the barn's doorway until he was sure Forrest was far away. Then he turned and looked up at the loft.

"Karma, let's get you somewhere where you feel safe. How about the sawmill? You can sit and think there about what you want to do next. I don't trust that guy."

Her head popped up over the stack of boards. "Okay," she said uncertainly. "Think it's safe now to come out?"

"Yeah," Peter replied with more confidence than he felt. He noticed Jake emerge from the cabin and walk toward the beach.

He turned and watched the small, backpack-clad figure scurry down the loft ladder inside their quarters. He led the way out the door toward the path. Within a few strides, however, he caught sight of Forrest running clumsily toward them from the woods.

"Quick," he hissed at Karma. "Jump on the Jet Ski!"

15   The Blind

Peter and Karma nearly knocked Jake over as they sprinted to the water.

"Karma!" Jake called out in surprise. He said it again as he turned to take in Forrest running toward them, boots thundering along the ground.

"Explain later," Peter shouted to Jake, pushing the Jet Ski the rest of the way into the water and leaping onto its saddle like a cowboy. The second he felt Karma's arms grip him, he tore away from shore, knowing that the splash and shout behind was Forrest falling in as he failed to grab Karma.

"What's going on?" he heard Jake ask, but a duo of raised voices—Forrest's and Jake's—was soon drowned out by the scream of the machine beneath him. He guessed that Forrest would probably grab Karma's bike and try to pursue them along the path beside shore. But Peter had other plans. Plans that involved getting to where the sawmill's river fed into Eagle Lake, before Forrest could.

As the little river came into view, Peter spun right and accelerated upstream. "Duck your head!" he ordered Karma as he did the same to avoid the low footbridge. A quick glance right revealed Forrest pedaling madly along the trail toward them. A smile flitted across Peter's face. The big man no more fit Karma's bicycle than a giant could race on a tricycle. And as long as Peter could keep the Jet Ski from hitting any underwater rocks, he and Karma would be miles beyond Forrest's reach in minutes. There was no path along the river; Forrest would need to do some perilous boulder hopping just to keep them in sight for the next few seconds.

"Peter, you're a crazy man," Karma shouted into his ear as he zigzagged up the river, dodging mid-river rocks. "Where're we going?"

"The sawmill," he responded. The machine bucked and splashed their legs as it worked its way up a wide tongue of water. They'd be lucky if they made it that far, of course, before the river got too choked. He didn't want to hurt Rocky's Jet Ski, or take the chance of plunging them into the current, even if it was slow-moving here. They had on neither life jackets nor helmets, and Karma was wearing a heavy backpack. Still, Peter was determined to put as much distance as possible between them and Forrest.

"Go, little Jet Ski, go," he thought, giving the machine as much throttle as he dared.

The Jet Ski's deafening noise was loud enough to scatter any birds or deer or squirrels long before Peter and Karma came around a river bend. And Peter felt a little bad about frightening them. But he was also reveling in the thrill of being a hero, sort of, and of steering the little craft on uncharted waters, sort of. He was tempted to try a quick jet turn, flicking it around at high speed, but there wasn't time for tricks even if they'd been wearing safety gear. And Rocky needed the craft in good condition.

His grip tightened and his knuckles went white as they approached a section steep enough to feature whitewater. Foam licked at the sides of undulating tongues, and sharp rocks stuck up like teeth. Peter gave it a fistful of throttle, chose his route, and ignored Karma's scream as they hurtled forward. For a few tense seconds, they tackled a powerful current, but halfway up, the Jet Ski was only treading water at full power.

"Oh man," Peter muttered. He backed off as slowly as he could, while feeling Karma's fingers all but puncturing his rib cage. The Jet Ski tottered a little, as if undecided whether to tip over to the left or the right. Then it skittered backwards like a water beetle that had decided to go with the flow.

Where the current they'd been fighting dumped into an eddy, the craft shuddered and whipped halfway around, but Peter's instincts told him which way to lean, and Karma was quick enough to lean with him.

"That was too close," Peter admitted as it steadied. He hopped out into knee-deep water beside shore.

"You can say that again," Karma said, sliding off the back end as if she expected the machine to buck her off if she didn't dismount quickly.

"But we're close to the mill and we've outrun Forrest," Peter said. He looked up to see a wall of weathered wood upstream. "Help me pull this up on shore, okay?"

Good thing Karma was strong for her size because it was a struggle hauling it to safety. Then, with frequent glances behind them, they scurried along the riverbank. When they came to the wooden wall Peter had spotted from below, he paused to inspect it. It was the wall of a giant tank the size and shape of a backyard swimming pool.

"Looks like some kind of holding tank," he said, pulling himself up high enough to peer in. It was filled with what looked like water. "The sawmill workers' after-work swimming pool?" he joked. "Phew! Smells like toilet cleaner. Definitely not for swimming in."

"It's called a dip tank," Karma said, pulling him away and hurrying upstream. "It used to be full of chemicals they dipped the lumber into before stacking it on the rail cars. Preserved the wood."

"Smells pretty toxic to me," Peter commented. "Hope no one ever fell in."

"Been empty for years," Karma said. "Shouldn't still smell."

Peter was going to tell her it wasn't empty, it was three-quarters full, but the girl was all but sprinting, and he decided to save his breath to keep up. He wasn't surprised when they ended up at the bird blind, by a different route than last time. She dumped her stuff on the floor, opened her pack, and pawed through its contents like a bum who'd discovered a dumpster.

"Food!" Her eyes sparkled as she examined the results of Peter's midnight kitchen raid. Her hands stopped as a plastic bag of corn dogs fell out.

"Corn dogs?"

"Yeah, last night's supper leftovers. They're actually pretty . . ."

"Peter, I'm vegetarian." Her hands lowered and her accusing eyes lifted to his. He felt totally, totally stupid.

"I knew that. I'm sorry. It was midnight, I was trying not to wake Rocky up, I wasn't thinking."

"Is there anything else in here?" She renewed an energetic digging through the pack. Out came doughnuts, cheese curls, cookies, a block of cheese. The wrapper was off the cheese and into her mouth before Peter could draw a breath. As some pieces crumbled off and fell to the floor, she kneeled, scooped them up, and popped them between her lips.

Peter stood and peered out the building's window, then its door. "Guess I'd better go," he said. "I'll come back later with more food."

"Okay," she said, but she was staring at the corn dogs in her hand. Slowly, she lifted them to her face, studied them like an archeologist who'd unearthed an unknown artifact, then bit into one.

Peter bit his tongue. Karma had just eaten meat. All 'cause he hadn't been thinking last night when he'd stuffed food in a getaway bag. What would Jake say? Now he'd corrupted her beyond any reason. Poor thing was so hungry she was willing to abandon the very last of her ideals. And if Forrest had hit her, it was half Peter's fault for asking to see the bird pipping, right? Peter hung his head as she looked at him while chewing.

"Not so different from tofu dogs," she finally ruled with a weak smile. "Next time bring ketchup."

"And vegetables. Not that Rocky ever buys them," Peter said sheepishly. "Guess Jake and I will have to take over writing up the grocery list."

"Good idea." She smiled.

"You'll be okay here?" he asked hesitantly.

"Got food, shelter, sleeping bag, and a million dollar view."

Peter glanced out the open-air window and saw an eagle alighting on a dead salmon beside the log pond.

"Hey, if you stuck around a little longer," she said with teasing eyes, "we could haul the Jet Ski into the log pond and I could launch off the log ramp on my wakeboard."

Peter chuckled, although he wasn't dead sure she was kidding. "Rocky could drive you to your friend's in Bellingham, you know."

"That's the first place Mom and Forrest will look for me. Here, I know too many hiding places for them to find me." She sounded almost cheerful, as if she was enjoying this. But he no longer felt okay about her rebellious streak.

"Karma?"

"Yup?"

"What does your mom see in Forrest?" Jake would say he had no right to ask. He knew he didn't. But it came out anyway. He watched her swallow her last bite of corn dog, wipe her mouth with the back of her hand, and stare at the abandoned sawmill.

"Guess she's been lonely a long time," Karma finally said, in a voice that sounded as if it was coming from a long way away. "And he was good at organizing the community and getting more money for our work, at first."

She drew her knees up to her chest and lowered her chin onto them.

Peter nodded. Made some sense. He took two steps toward the door and looked around to take in her tiny figure huddled in a corner of the drafty hideaway.

"What you really wanted to ask, though, was what he sees in her," she said.

Peter straightened and felt a patch of red creep up his neck. Had he been thinking that?

She raised a hand and gestured out the window at the sawmill. "The answer is land. If not this land, then the plot nearest it."

Peter shifted from one foot to another. He hesitated, carefully measuring his next words.

"Skye came over last night looking for you. She's taking this pretty hard, you know."

Karma shrugged, lowered her eyes.

"She said if we saw you, we were supposed to tell you that Forrest is in Bellingham for a couple of days. So I'm guessing she has no idea he was hanging around the cabin looking for you this morning. And I'm guessing he's not going back to the commune today."

Karma raised her eyes, which revealed no surprise. She said nothing.

"Skye thought maybe if you knew he was in Bellingham, you might come home."

"I'm not going home yet!" she said, eyes flashing.

Peter nodded slowly, but he wasn't ready to give up. "Maybe without Forrest there, you guys can work it out. I hate to see your mom so worried. I kind of feel like some of this is my fault."

"It's not your fault and it's not your business, and don't you dare tell her where I am!" Karma commanded, backing away from him as if she no longer trusted him.

Oh no, now he'd blown it. "I'm sorry..." he began.

"Whatever," she said dismissively, taking yet another step backwards. "Thanks for the food. You can go now."

Peter checked his watch, then let his eyes roam over her bruised face again. Should he ask her about it? Nah. If she wanted to talk to him about it, she would. He wouldn't push her. He sighed and nodded. "Guess I'd better get outta here before Forrest comes looking anyway."

"Bye, Peter. Thanks for the food and the ride." Her voice had softened a little, but her face was hard, her eyes suspicious. "I'll be fine."

16   Peter Returns

Jake was speechless as Peter sped away. How could Peter have hidden Karma in their loft without Jake knowing about it? How long had she been there? How dare his best friend not tell him what was going on! And how dare he steal Rocky's Jet Ski and stop Forrest from being able to talk to Karma, or take her back to the commune. Her mom must be sick with worry.

If she'd run away from home, the last thing Peter should be doing was interfering. In fact, the more Jake thought about it, the more furious he became. Teaching Karma wakeboarding and video games was one thing. But Peter had just crossed a serious line, in Jake's opinion.

He watched Forrest get off Karma's bike by the bridge and shake a fist toward the escaping pair. Then the big man turned. Even from that distance, the glare with which he fixed Jake made Jake shudder.

Jake's discomfort grew as the man and his bike turned around and headed back to where Jake stood.

"Where'd they go?" he growled as he let the bike drop and moved toward Jake.

"I don't know. Honest, Forrest, I had no idea she was here!" Jake found himself saying. "Peter never let on!"

Jake winced as the big, bearded man took another step closer and placed his face close to Jake's. His eyes were flashing with rage.

"Do I have to call the police, or are you going to tell me where Peter has taken her? Because her mother and I are worried, and we can't talk things out with Karma if you're hiding her."

Jake took a step back. He might be tall for his age, but next to Forrest, he felt like a stump.

"Tell me!" came the next roar. Jake felt as if he was half submerged in the lake, one wrist handcuffed to one tow-rope handle, the other to another, with two boats pointed in opposite directions about to pull him up. He was mad at Peter, and thought Karma should get home, but he also needed a chance to talk to his buddy before he gave anything away. Karma had looked just fine the brief glance he'd had of her, but maybe there was a reason she was trying to get away from Forrest, and a reason that Peter had hidden her and was helping her?

He could guess where Peter had taken Karma: to the bird blind. And he also remembered something Skye had said last night: that Forrest had gone to Bellingham for a couple of days. Something about this wasn't adding up. Why had Forrest lied?

"Speak!"

Jake noticed that the man's fists were clenched at his sides.

"I think I know where Peter took her," Jake said, thinking fast. "Is there a road from the sawmill to Bellingham?"

"Yes," Forrest responded. "It's a more direct route than from here or our community."

"And doesn't she have a friend in Bellingham?"

"Yes. Crystal. She used to live in the community with her parents until they moved last month. We called them as soon as we realized Karma was missing. She's not there."

Jake shrugged. "Well, like I said, I didn't know Karma was here last night, but I heard Peter talking to someone after I went to bed." He was making that last bit up, but he felt a need to look as if he was on Forrest's side and yet throw Forrest off the idea that she was hiding at the sawmill. If he sent Forrest on a wild goose chase into Bellingham, he could buy some time to talk to Peter and Karma and find out what was up. "I thought he was talking to Rocky. I figured they were whispering 'cause they thought I was asleep. All I heard was 'friend in Bellingham' and 'sawmill road.' My guess is he's taking her up the river to that road, so she can walk to Bellingham and stay with her friend—Crystal. I don't think Peter should have, honest. But he doesn't listen to me." Jake didn't need to fake the bitterness in his voice on the last two lines.

Forrest's fiery eyes squinted at Jake, then he unballed his fists. "Okay. I'll drive Skye into town so those two can talk." He glanced toward the footbridge. "Teenagers," he finished lamely, as if trying to convince Jake it was all a trivial incident, and as if forgetting that Jake was one, too.

"Want a lift home on Hoochie's Ride?" Jake offered.

Forrest looked at Jake with a startled expression, then shook his head and tugged at the end of his beard. "Nope, I need the exercise," he ruled. "Thanks anyway. Sorry for the trouble that Karma's causing." With that, he ambled away, boots stepping heavily on the path.

Jake watched him until the trees swallowed him up just past the footbridge. There, he paused to look up the river, still tugging at his beard.

Jake sighed and climbed into Hoochie's Ride with hammer, boards, and pieces of an old foam mattress in hand. He was still bent over the engine an hour later when the scream of the Jet Ski shattered the quiet of the lake.

Jake raised his head, saw Peter power down the last bit of river and catch a bit of air where it joined the lake, like he was some kind of stuntman. Well, at least he hadn't hurt the machine on the river rocks. Or been stopped by Forrest. Karma, of course, was no longer on the craft. Jake ground his teeth as Peter approached.

"Hey, Jake." Peter looked around a little nervously. "Did Forrest leave?" His manner was definitely uneasy, but as far as Jake was concerned, he wasn't looking as guilty as Jake figured he should be.

Jake laid down his hammer and fixed Peter with a glare. "Disappeared. Gone back to the commune to report what you've just done—if not to call the police on you."

"Did he ask where I was taking her? Did you tell him?" Peter's face held a hint of concern.

Jake crossed his arms. "Maybe, maybe not. Tell me what's going on right now."

Peter nodded, hauled the Jet Ski up the shore, looked about, and motioned Jake into the cabin.

"I need some refueling." He fixed the two of them some hot cocoa and wandered out to the front porch to sink into a big chair. Jake took the hammock. There, to the background chirps of birds and the buzz of crickets, Peter spilled the entire story. Jake was taken aback to hear about the bruise on Karma's face.

"I didn't notice it. You sure Forrest hit her? Did you ask her?"

"No, she was pretty defensive about everything, and I figured she'd probably just lie, anyway."

"Maybe, but you don't know he hit her." Jake lowered his mug and ran his eyes up the long, thick trunk of the tree near the cabin that held an eagle's nest. He wondered how the tangled mess of sticks up there managed to form a home.

"So what did you tell Forrest?" Peter asked warily.

"I told him you'd taken her up the river so she could walk into Bellingham on the river road. I'm glad I didn't tell Forrest where she was, Peter, but I still don't like it. We should probably take Hoochie's Ride over to the commune and tell Skye and Rocky right away."

Peter sighed. "Not yet. She got pretty mad at me when I told her that her mom was worried about her. She just wants some time on her own. I figure she needs it, don't you? Let's hike up there to give her some more food. Maybe you can do a better job of trying to talk her into going home."

Jake heard an eagle's slow wings beat over the lake. He lifted his head to watch it approach the nest high overhead, a fish in its talons. He might have been imagining things, but he thought the soft peep of an eaglet drifted down to where he and Peter sat. He watched the mother flapping on the nest's rim. He wondered how long it would be before the eaglet rose to perch on that rim, pumping her own wings, ready to try her first flight. He wondered how eaglets knew when they were ready to leave the nest. Did they get a signal from their parents? For sure, some must hurt themselves taking the leap before they are ready. Jake shrugged. Just nature, he guessed.

"Okay," he agreed. "Soon as I'm done with the job Rocky assigned me."

"Perfect. I'm going to try out that new computer game," Peter said, rising and walking inside. "What you up to on Hoochie's Ride, anyway?"

"Building a box over the engine to dampen the sound."

"Yeah? That'll make Skye a little happier. Maybe the eagles, too. Your idea or Rocky's?"

"Rocky's."

Peter disappeared inside. But before Jake was out of the hammock, Peter called out, "Jake, get a load of this stuff in the printer tray, things Rocky's been printing out."

Thinking it might have to do with the engine-dampening project Rocky had assigned him,

Jake strolled into the cabin. He bent over Peter's shoulders.

"Bluewater Network. What's that? And something from the National Parks Conservation Association," Jake said.

"Read them."

"Before 1990, emissions of personal water craft, also known as PWCs, Jet Skis, or Sea-Doos, were unregulated in the United States. Many were powered by two-stroke engines, which are smaller and lighter than four-stroke engines but much more polluting."

"Not the technical stuff," Peter objected.

"A 100-horsepower PWC doing doughnuts off-shore makes more pollution in one hour than a car creates in ten years of driving. Whoa." Jake paused. "More pollution in one hour than a car creates in ten years? That's incredible. Sure doesn't sound like something Rocky would download though."

"Not before Hoochie died, anyway," Peter agreed.

Jake wondered. Was Rocky secretly researching whether his Jet Skis really might be poisoning the lake? Might have contributed to Hoochie's death?

"The high frequency sounds also startle birds, causing them to fly away from their nests and leave their eggs vulnerable to predators."

Jake thought about the dead eaglet Skye had brought over, which Karma had buried.

"Two-strokes disturb wildlife and discharge a shocking one-third of their fuel and oil unburned into the water and air. Every year, PWCs pollute America's water as much as four major oil spills. This puts toxins into the food chain."

"Yuck! Four oil spills? But since when does Rocky worry about the food chain?" Peter interrupted with a guffaw as his hand dove into a bowl of potato chips.

"The federal government should require quieter and less polluting four-stroke engines," Jake said, continuing to read.

"Rocky's are old two-strokes, right?" Peter asked Jake.

"Yeah. Can't believe he's reading this stuff. Think that's why he hasn't been using the Jet Skis?" Jake pondered.

"And why he asked you to quiet down Hoochie's Ride?"

Jake shrugged. "Hey, this is snooping in his stuff. Get back to your computer game. I'm gonna get back to the boat. When I'm finished, we're eating lunch and then hiking to the sawmill, right?"

"Aye, aye, captain. Speaking of food, what're you making for lunch? Can you cook something vegetarian so we can take it to Karma?"

Jake smiled. "You're in luck. I made Rocky buy broccoli and carrots and some healthy things yesterday. He was so disgusted he put them in the fridge's bottom drawer so he wouldn't have to look at them."

"No way! Guess that's how I missed them when I was raiding the kitchen for Karma last night. Bet Rocky won't touch that stuff."

"Hey, if someone who once fished with dynamite can start worrying about two-stroke engine pollution, he can eat broccoli, too."

"I'm not betting on it," his buddy answered, placing Rocky's printouts carefully back into the printer tray.

17   A Search

"**D**on't like the look of the sky," Jake commented as they hopped from boulder to boulder along the river after lunch, their packs full of food for Karma.

"Me either," Peter returned.

Jake looked up at the sky, wiped his brow, and tasted the salt of sweat on his lips. It looked like it could rain.

"Shhh," he cautioned as he heard twigs cracking in the undergrowth. Then he saw a bird hopping along the ground where the sound had come from. He lowered his voice. "Wonder if we should keep quiet, in case Forrest is around here looking for Karma?" He still felt unsure about interfering in a family fight, and he was still annoyed with Peter for helping Karma escape. But if Forrest was violent, they needed to be careful. The real reason Jake had agreed to come was to take one shot at persuading Karma to return before Rocky and Skye got police involved.

"Good idea. He's probably figured out by now she's not in Bellingham," Jake said, glancing around into the shadows of the giant cedars. He lifted some strands of Spanish moss that hung like cobwebs between trees. "Wonder if he really went back to the commune and drove Skye into town."

"You'd have seen his truck along the lake while I was dropping Karma off, right?"

"True. I never did. Plus, Rocky would've come home if Forrest showed there." The notion of Rocky and Skye working together to organize a search team was hard enough to fathom. Forrest joining them was way too much of a stretch.

They went silent then, trudging, looking behind, pausing now and again to listen for anyone who might be following them. It was pretty difficult to tell, of course, what with all the birds scuttling about in the bushes.

Jake halted when Peter stopped and raised his hand. He craned his head to look past Peter's arm and noticed a large wooden oval tank—kind of like a backyard swimming pool—near overgrown railway tracks. It was a feature he hadn't noticed when Karma had shown them the place. Then again, the area seemed full of falling-down outbuildings and abandoned machinery.

Peter, apparently satisfied, crept ahead, keeping on the outskirts of the clearing. Jake, curious and spotting a ladder attached to the side of the tank, raised a foot to it and lifted his chin up and over the tank's rim.

Some kind of water supply, he decided at first, looking at the clear liquid dotted by floating pine needles. Then he scrunched up his nose. It smelled vaguely like disinfectant. The stuff his mom made him clean the bathroom with every weekend.

He lowered himself one step and saw Peter signaling him over. But he hung there for a moment, scratching his head. If the mill had been shut down for twenty years, anything in an open tank would have evaporated off long ago. It made no sense for anything to be in there but dirty rainwater. He pulled himself back up, held his mouth firmly shut, and breathed deeply through his nostrils.

Yikes! His nose and throat stung as if they were on fire. He gasped as he turned his head away to stop the burning.

This was definitely not water. Which meant that any squirrel that fell in, or bird that mistook it for a bird bath, would probably die a quick death. He thought for a second, then unscrewed the cap to his water bottle and poured out its water. He unbuckled his belt, fastened the water bottle on the end of the belt, and lowered the belt to the tank. When he'd managed to collect a sample of the stuff, he pulled it up. He knew better than to grab the bottle with his bare hands. Instead, he pulled a sweatshirt from his backpack and used its hood as a glove to replace the cap super-tightly and wipe down the bottle and belt. Whoa! Where his arm brushed against an unwiped portion of the bottle just for a second, an angry rash formed. Powerful stuff, this chemical. Maybe Rocky would know what it was. His dad had owned the place, after all.

He jumped down, intending to sprint over to an impatient-looking Peter, when his ankle half-buckled in a muddy groove. He bent down to rub it, then hesitated. The groove was fresh and looked like the imprint of a tractor tire. Hadn't Karma said the new owner was a rancher who ignored this piece of his land? Wait. She'd said she had seen tractor tire marks. Probably him checking up on the place.

Jake looked over to Peter, saw him standing with hands on his hips, silently mouthing the words "hurry up."

Okay, okay, Jake thought. Ears fully perked, eyes following the tractor tire ruts back toward the saw-mill, Jake walked as silently as he could to where Peter was waiting at the edge of the clearing.

"That's not water!" Peter hissed, grabbing the water bottle from Jake. "You'll die if you drink whatever's in there!"

"I know!" Jake replied, trying to grab it back from where Peter held it out of his reach. "And I know I can never use that bottle again for drinking water. I just thought maybe Rocky could tell us what it is and why it's there. It's an open tank. Got to be bad for the animals around here. Maybe he can talk the rancher into draining it."

Peter rolled his eyes. "What are you, an en-vi-ron-mental officer?" Jake noticed he pronounced it sarcastically, just like Rocky and that waitress back in Arizona. Jake was trying to figure out how to reply when a mighty splash from the log pond the other side of the sawmill prompted the two boys to crouch down behind a tree.

Heart beating fast, Jake listened as a panicked splashing continued. Had to be an animal or person. But if something or someone was drowning, they weren't crying out.

Jake looked at Peter, whose face registered alarm. Karma could swim, Jake reminded himself. She'd grown up swimming in Eagle Lake. She wouldn't be flailing around like that if she'd slipped in. A grim image entered his brain: Forrest leaping out from a hiding place and pushing an unsuspecting Karma underwater before she could cry out. A giant-sized, murderous bully seeing an opportunity to finish her off without witnesses.

Okay, that was silly. Just because Forrest was a sort of control freak didn't mean he was out to murder anyone. Still, before Peter could object, Jake sprinted to the underbelly of the sawmill, his head down like a soldier expecting unfriendly fire. He hit the dirt where he'd have a closer view: behind a stone footing the size of a large boulder. From here, the splashing in the pond was so loud he thought he could feel droplets hitting his face. He slithered a little forward, stomach on dirt, trying to glimpse the source of the noise. Big, panicked eyes locked on his as hooves shot out of the water.

A deer! Fallen between logs in the pond. It had probably walked out on a log from shore with no clue the logs could spin with no notice. Poor thing was sure to drown if the boys didn't help. As Jake rose to make his way toward the struggling animal, Peter sprinted ahead of him, Jake's water bottle slapping his thigh from a carabiner on his belt. He ran out onto the biggest log as if he was one of those lumberjacks who entertain audiences by testing how long they can stay on a spinning log with spiked boots.

"Peter!" Jake called out in warning as his buddy wavered and spilled in beside the deer.

Trying not to laugh, Jake ran forward and tackled the shore end of the log to hold it steady so it wouldn't swivel as his soaked friend grabbed on.

Peter's grip moved the log away from the thrashing yearling. The panicked animal swam till it could raise its spindly legs to the shore and took off. Jake watched its wet, white rump bouncing with each step.

"Peter, you okay?" Jake asked as he extended an arm to help Peter out.

"Just good and wet," he said sheepishly. "Good thing you had the food pack."

"Wonder where Karma is," Jake commented. If she'd seen that, she'd have emerged giggling.

The two boys scanned the entire property.

"Karma!" Peter called out.

The only sound was birds and the wind in the trees.

"Maybe she's moved. Maybe she doesn't trust us anymore. Or me, anyway," Peter said, his face a study in misery. "Let's at least drop the food off."

Jake nodded and they trekked around the pond to the bird blind. It was empty, even the space beneath the floorboards. Jake's heart felt heavy.

"She might've gone back home already," Jake ventured, knowing it was unlikely.

"She might have found a new place to hide. Or Forrest might've gotten here first," Peter said, head hung low.

"Or she might be nearby watching us, just playing it safe," Jake said hopefully.

Before Peter could respond to that, the sound of an approaching engine made the boys' eyes widen.

"A tractor engine. Must be the guy who owns the place," Jake said.

Peter nodded, swiveling his head toward the river up which they'd come. "You take the near side of the river. I'll take the far side. Look for Karma along the way. Maybe she'll answer you, not me. Meet you back at the cabin in an hour."

"Good plan," Jake responded. "See you there."

He watched Peter sprint around the log pond as the sound of the engine drew nearer. He himself made it to the far end of the sawmill. But as he hovered in its shadow, ready to dash across the final clearing to the river, the tractor burst into view.

Jake, not wanting to get in trouble for trespassing, figured it was safer to hide under the sawmill till the rancher left.

The diesel motor grew louder as Jake stumbled through the lower maze of the sawmill. He ducked under belts that rose to the main floor. He crawled past iron wheels he could have stood inside, from toes to upward reaching fingertips. He knocked over an oiling can as he brushed past chains with links the size of his palm. Finally, he dove for cover in the boiler room. Despite the coolness of the dark space, he was sweating. He flattened himself between the wall and the huge, rusty boiler tank. Not much chance the rancher will get off that tractor and troop through the sawmill's lower corridors looking for someone, he told himself. He closed his nostrils to the room's noxious oily odor.

Two dots of cloud-dimmed daylight fell on him like laser pointers. One came from a fist-sized hole in a floorboard just above his head. The other shone from the hollow center of a knothole in the wood of the wall beside him. He bent down to press his eye to the wall peephole. It framed a view of the dip tank.

The loud put-put was definitely a tractor, Jake decided. A rattle, bumping, and thudding indicated that the tractor was pulling a load of something not tightly tied down, in some kind of trailer. The ground beneath Jake shook as the tractor pulled up beside the sawmill. Diesel fumes mixed with the boiler room's overpowering smells. Jake's stomach tightened.

As he kept his sweaty brow pressed to the peep-hole, the tractor's bottom half came into view, accompanied by a screech of brakes. Jake lifted his hands to press over his ears. It was a tractor, alright. A green one with patches of rust on its underbelly. The hitch between it and its trailer was within spitting distance. If he craned his head just so, he could see a couple of small logs in the trailer, the items that had been jostling about during the tractor's approach. He saw a flash of someone jumping down from the driver's seat. Now he could see the bottom half of a tall male driver in jeans and boots unloading the logs. Strange that he was by himself, Jake thought. Hadn't Karma said it took two dozen people to run the sawmill? That, of course, was assuming the owner was starting it up again. Or maybe the fellow was a trespasser. If so, that would make four of us, Jake mused, wiping sweat from his forehead.

He jumped as the first log hit the floor directly over his head. Had the guy really hoisted it up there? Must be a former world champion weightlifter, or have a good workers' compensation injury policy. Those logs had to weigh a hundred pounds each.

Wham. The second one landed over his head, making the wall against which his forehead was leaning shudder. Dust filtered down the hole above as a third and fourth log slid onto the old sawmill floor, making him want to sneeze. He held his breath.

The man's knees were so close to Jake's peephole that if the opening were larger, Jake could have reached out and untied his bootlaces. Instead, he shrank against the cold boiler as the boots leapt up to the floor over his head. He hardly dared look at the hole for fear of an eyeball peering back.

He jumped as something slammed overhead and cringed at a dragging sound. Then a roar sent his hands to his ears. Both the tractor and a saw had come to life, the tractor's motor powering the saw, he guessed. As ripping, whizzing sounds deafened him, sawdust snowed down on Jake's hair.

Finally, some mighty thuds sounded as the man tossed the freshly sawn wood pieces down into the tractor's trailer. When he heard the man jump down onto the tractor and rumble toward the dip tank, Jake applied his eye to the peephole once again.

No way, Jake thought. What is Forrest doing here?

He watched Forrest's muscular form heft what looked like newly made fence posts into the chemical bath. A kind of wood preservative, Jake guessed.

Some environmentalist, Jake thought. The guy pretended to be fanatical about saving eagles, and here he was sneaking around to use the sawmill his father had managed and using toxic-smelling stuff right beside a river leading into Eagle Lake.

Toxic. Another word for poison. The word made Jake flash back to the graves of Hoochie and the eagle, and the dead salmon on the shores of the lake. He felt for his water bottle, the one with the sample of liquid. Gone! Then he remembered Peter snatching it from him to stop him drinking from it.

Jake gazed out at Forrest again. The man was

walking back toward the sawmill while the logs soaked. Jake raised his hand to brush sawdust from his hair.

"Achoo!" He couldn't believe he'd just sneezed. "Achoo!"

Jake froze, heart pounding.

He pressed his eye back to the peephole. Oh-oh. Forrest's eyes were locked on the boiler room. Jake crouched down well below the hole.

"Karma?" Forrest's voice coaxed from where the tractor had stood only half an hour earlier. It was a coax, yes, but one with a note of surprise, maybe even alarm, Jake thought.

Jake held his breath.

"Hello?" Forrest called out again, less certain. Jake heard the big man's boots crunch gravel as he moved closer.

"I said who's there?" Forrest demanded.

Jake, heart in his throat, shrank even farther down the board against which Forrest was now leaning.

"Karma? Your mother and I have been worried sick. We've been looking for you. Let me give you a lift home, okay?"

Ha! Now he was trying a friendlier voice. Wasn't very good at that, Jake decided.

"Whatever," came Forrest's voice again, a new voice that sounded as if it had just taken a tumble into the same acidic bath he'd given the logs. He directed the word deliberately through the hole from which Jake had been spying. His breath all but parted the hairs on the top of Jake's head. But Jake knew he was out of view.

The boots crunched away from the wall as the first raindrops pinged against the corrugated roof of the sawmill. After a moment, the rain's staccato was drowned out by Forrest's tractor roaring back to life.

Jake leapt up and flew out of the boiler room. He ran through the sawmill's undermaze, looking for another dark space to hide, one that Forrest didn't suspect. First he chose a place behind a pillar. But after five minutes of crouching there, he decided to look for a better hiding spot. Wandering to the far end of the mill, the end closest to the dip tank, he spotted the perfect place: a closet in the back of a drafty, cobwebby room. He slipped in, fingers groping in the dark. His hands scanned the far wall, checking for protruding nails before he trusted himself to lean his back against it. His nose picked up a smell that sent his heart racing. Before his brain could process a warning, however, his fingers touched something fleshy and warm.

Jake cried out and jumped back, but not before a strong set of hands closed around his neck.

18   Return to the Commune

Once he had reached the far side of the river, Peter ran as fast and as silently as he could. He loved foot races, especially against Jake. He had every intention of getting to the cabin first. Still soaked from his log-pond dunking, he also couldn't wait to change clothes. When he found a big boulder to duck behind, he paused to catch his breath just for a second. Judging from the sounds of the diesel engine, the tractor had pulled into the clearing beside the sawmill. He craned his neck hoping he could see it. Even from this distance, he recognized the tall figure on it immediately and drew in his breath.

"Well, Jake old buddy," he mumbled under his breath, "guess you're going to beat me to the cabin, 'cause I have to stick around here another minute to see what Forrest is up to. Where'd he get that tractor, anyway?"

It was a rusty old thing and pulling a trailer of jostling logs. Peter observed Forrest heaving the logs up onto the floor of the sawmill as if they were matchsticks. The guy was strong, that's for sure. He heard the high-pitched whine of a saw cutting the logs, then watched in amazement as Forrest drove what looked like fence posts over to the dip tank and dunked them in. Made it look as easy and natural as plopping a banana into chocolate dip at an ice cream parlor.

Hey! Did he have permission to be here? What was this, a side business? Did Karma know he came here? Surely she'd have said if she'd seen him here before. And Peter would bet a million dollars that no one at the commune knew their fearless leader was messing with logs, saws, and chemicals on someone else's property when they thought he was doing business in Bellingham.

He watched Forrest wander back to the sawmill, stand beside an outer wall talking to himself for a minute, then walk back and hop onto his tractor to fire it up. By then, Peter had seen enough. He decided to retrace his steps to the bird blind and warn Karma if she was there.

"Karma!" he whispered as he drew near the blind. No answer. Glancing behind him, he descended the stairs and poked his head beneath the floorboards. No Karma, and no pack. Hey! That meant she'd taken the pack of food they'd left her! So she was around! She had been here. She was probably watching Forrest right now from some other hiding place. She was smart and sneaky, that girl, and knew the best hiding places all around the mill. No way was Forrest going to catch her.

"Karma," he whispered one more time. He felt sad that she seemed not to trust the boys anymore, that she was staying hidden and refusing to respond. Then again, maybe it wasn't safe for him to be looking for her when Forrest was so close. Peter decided he'd better get going. He had to catch up with Jake and let him know he'd seen Forrest here. Then they had to find Rocky and report what they'd seen, and get over to the commune to let Skye know that Karma was safe—that no one needed a search party or the police.

As he left the bird blind and retraced his steps along the river, raindrops splattered Peter's face. He was surprised to see that Forrest hadn't left after all. His tractor, still idling, was empty, and there was no sign of Forrest from where Peter stood. All the more reason, Peter figured, to get gone fast, especially since the rain on his wet clothing was making him shiver. Besides, if he didn't get to the cabin soon, Jake would worry.

He jumped from boulder to boulder along the river, glancing back frequently. Several times he called Karma's name softly. There was no sound but the musical tinkle of the river—clear water splashing and playing in its rush down to Eagle Lake. He was tempted to dip his cupped hands in for a drink, but just because it looked clear didn't make it safe, he knew. He touched the water bottle filled with that evil-smelling liquid still lashed to his belt. Maybe Jake had been clever, after all, to collect that. It'd be interesting to get it tested.

Forrest must've filled that tank for dipping fence posts, he reasoned. Maybe Forrest was the one who'd put up that "weatherproof fence posts" sign beside the Bellingham bus station that Peter had seen, the one with the cellphone number. The number from which Rocky had never gotten an answer. Peter grinned a sardonic grin. As if Forrest would return a call from Rocky, even to sell him fence posts. Rocky was Forrest's imagined enemy, the one who had sold "his" sawmill out from under him. Well, as it turned out, Forrest was working that sawmill after all, making it his on the sly, probably helping support the commune with it. Fence posts probably pay more than artwork, Peter mused. And Forrest probably figures that what Skye doesn't know won't hurt her.

Well, she was going to know, and so was Rocky, as soon as Peter could get to the cabin and then to the commune. Just thinking of the commune made him hungry for a minute. Their food was pretty good, considering it was vegetarian. Maybe Tao would fix him up something when he got there. He rubbed his rumbling stomach. He rushed from the bridge down to the path and sprinted the final distance to the cabin in the downpour.

"Jake!" he shouted.

No answer. He ran from the cabin to the barn to the boathouse. He noticed the Jet Skis gone from the boathouse.

"Jake? Rocky?" One of them had been back if the Jet Skis were gone. He noticed that the boat trailer was gone, too. So Rocky had returned and driven off with the Jet Skis. What did that mean? Had Jake gone with him? Peter searched for a note, found none. He walked to the barn and changed clothes, then returned to the cabin and waited around for a while. He microwaved himself the last corn dog.

It made him think of Karma, hiding up at the sawmill in what had turned into pelting rain. Maybe Jake had found her? Had been delayed by talking with her? Hey, maybe he'd talked her into going home, and they'd walked straight to the commune!

Peter looked out the cabin window at Hoochie's Ride—the new, quieter Hoochie's Ride, thanks to Jake's mechanical smarts. That's it. He'd leave a note for Jake and Rocky and drive the Malibu over to the commune. With any luck, everyone would be there celebrating Karma's return.

He left a note on the center of the table and grabbed a raincoat. After a moment's hesitation, he decided to take the water bottle of wood preservative, too. On his way across the lake, he thought about pulling some doughnuts, then remembered that article about how much pollution that maneuver causes. He wished Hoochie were keeping him company—paws above the dashboard, pink tongue hanging out, red bandanna collecting the raindrops.

As he pulled alongside the commune's dock, Skye emerged, her hair tangled and rain-soaked. Her eyes searched the boat as if it wasn't Peter she was expecting. One look at her face and Peter knew Karma was still missing. Tao appeared and helped Peter tie up.

"Rocky's gone into town to check a few places for Karma," Tao said before Peter could speak. "He helped us look all morning. We're heading out again in half an hour. Have any news for us?"

Peter turned to Skye's long face. "Jake and I were up at the sawmill this morning. We didn't find her, but she's there."

"Karma's at the sawmill?" she exclaimed. "How do you know? Did you talk to her? Is she okay?"

"We didn't find her, but we left her some food

and it disappeared when we weren't looking," Peter responded. "Forrest is there, too."

"Forrest?" Skye interjected. "He's in Bellingham! But did you see Karma? Do you know why she left, and whether she's okay?"

"Come in out of this rain, and let me fix you some hot chai," Tao offered.

Once settled with the hot, sweetened drink in the lodge, Peter started to spill his story to Skye, Tao, and gathered commune members. He told them how Karma had shown up in the middle of the night, and how he'd decided to take her to the sawmill when he'd seen her face the next morning.

"She got that bruise falling from the last rope ladder at the bottom of the eagle platform tree," Tao interrupted. "Forrest would never hit Karma."

"She unhitched her safety carabiner a couple of feet too soon when we were coming down," Skye added, nodding. "That's why we grounded her, Forrest and me."

Peter looked from Skye to Tao to the community members standing around.

"She was in too much of a hurry. Didn't follow the safety rules," confirmed a woman with hair that reached to the small of her back. "She didn't tell you Forrest hit her, did she?"

Peter hung his head. "No," he mumbled. "I guess

I shouldn't have assumed, or taken her up to the sawmill."

Skye crossed her arms and gave Peter a withering look. "But she didn't object to the idea, did she? And did you go up the river with no lifejackets or helmets on?"

Peter nodded and hung his head again.

"How do we find her and get her back?" Skye asked, her face creased with worry again.

"Wait, Skye. I think he has more to his story, right?" Tao encouraged Peter.

Peter snuck a forkful of yogurt and creamcheese pie from the dish Tao had brought him before speaking again. He related the story of Forrest appearing on the tractor, and sawing and dipping what looked like fence posts.

"Fence posts?" Skye repeated in surprise, directing her gaze out the lodge's window to a small pile of fence posts.

"Fence posts," Peter confirmed, then reached for the water bottle and unclipped it from his belt. "This is the stuff from the dip tank."

Skye took it, unscrewed the lid gingerly, and passed her nose over the top like she was choosing perfume in a department store. Her eyes bugged out as she yanked it away from her nose.

"Careful," she said as she passed it to Tao. "That's

not what Dad had in the dip tank when the mill was running," she said. "I was only fifteen when it shut down, but I know what he had in there wasn't that strong. This stuff smells deadly!"

Tao was careful to hold the container much further from his nose than Skye had. Cautiously, he took a small sniff, looked thoughtful, and sniffed again. "Pentachlorophenol," he said, eyes widening in astonishment. "A fungicide that's been banned for years!"

"What's a fungicide?" Peter ventured, "and how do you know just by smelling?" Tao was a cook, not a scientist, right?

Skye and Tao grinned together.

"It's a wood preservative," Skye replied. "Tao worked at an oceanside sawmill in California—like, what, forty years ago?" she explained, smiling at Tao as his gray Afro bobbed agreement. "And cooks have good noses."

Tao plucked a black, felt-tipped pen from a nearby shelf and drew a skull and crossbones on the water bottle. "We can get the Environmental Protection Agency to test this in a lab," Tao said, "but I'll bet my life on it." He tightened the top on the water bottle. "Skye, your grandfather probably used it in that dip tank before it was banned. Forrest might have found a very old container of it in some shed up there. The stuff's deadly. Breathe it in too much and it can kill you. Get a little on a hand with an open cut, and it can kill you. And if that old dip tank ever sprang a leak and it ran into the river . . ."

". . . fish and eagles and dogs might be poisoned?" Peter finished for him.

There was a startled silence as Skye, Tao, and Peter exchanged looks. "Yes," Tao answered soberly, turning disturbed eyes out the window to the lake.

"Since you've been so honest with us, Peter, I'll share something with you," Skye said in a grave voice.

Peter watched Tao lift empty plates and head into the kitchen. The commune members began studying the floor.

"After Forrest and I grounded Karma for being careless on the rope ladder, she called Forrest some terrible names." Skye paused as if to collect herself.

Peter waited.

"She blames him for people leaving our community, and for me not . . . well, anyway. She said if he and I really believed in love, honesty, patience, tolerance, equality, and respect for the earth"—here Skye gazed at the water bottle of pentachlorophenol Tao had set on the table—"we would let the members of our community vote on whether he should be a member."

She shifted her eyes to the eagle she had carved. "Everyone else here was voted on, but I brought Forrest in without a vote." She rubbed her left ring finger. Peter noticed that she'd removed her engagement ring.

"And he kind of took over?" Peter suggested gently.

Skye turned and looked at Peter as if she'd forgotten for a moment he was there. Then her eyes clouded and she nodded slowly. "After she said that, Karma stormed off. But I realized she was right. So I told Forrest we would hold a vote. And that became a fight, and I told him he and I were finished, and then he left."

Tears were slipping down Skye's face now. Peter was glad when Tao returned and put a hand on her shoulder. Skye raised an arm to wipe her tears away and seemed to pull herself together.

"And then we had a vote." She paused. "And neither Karma nor Forrest knows the results—yet." She sank down in a willow-branch chair and slowly raised her eyes to the skull and crossbones label Tao had drawn. "Or maybe Forrest does without being told."

19   Chase

Jake, unable to breathe for the thick arm around his neck, did what anyone would do in the same situation: He bent forward and chomped his teeth down hard on the hairy flesh.

His assailant cried out and loosened the stranglehold just long enough for Jake to yank free. Now Jake was running, his feet tearing along the dim corridors. He could hear Forrest's heavy breathing behind him but knew the big man in his heavy boots was a poor match for a fleet-footed boy in runners. He dodged here and there beneath the footings, trying to remember where the stairs were. The patter of his feet against the sawdust-coated ground matched the rhythm of the rain now pelting the tin roof of the sawmill upstairs. When he came to the stairs, Jake bolted up them.

"Jake!" Forrest called out, a hint of surprise in his panting voice. "Jake! No need to run! Sorry I scared you! I didn't know it was you. I thought it was a thief or a vandal."

Yeah, right, Jake thought. And I thought you were an environmentalist commune hippie. He reached the top of the steps and paused, not knowing whether to leap over machinery or dash down the ramp and run out onto a floating log. An image of Forrest and him spinning logs until someone fell in gave him a fleeting smile. Then again, Forrest, he reminded himself, had grown up here and was wearing boots. He just might be all too nimble on logs.

As raindrops from a leak in the roof hit his face, and Forrest's boots thudded on the steps behind him, Jake took a flying leap across the log carriage. But the rain had transformed the sawdust on the floor and the slick metal of the carriage plates. Jake's shoes slid like ice skates out from under him, and he went flying. He yelled as he landed and felt something sharp slice into his left arm. Then he lay still, head scrunched against the far wall, eyes looking up to the lever Karma had said would start the machinery going.

Forrest, paused on the other side of the carriage, sounded alarmed. "Jake! Are you okay? You've cut your arm on the saw blade! Don't move! I'm coming to help."

Jake tried to roll over, but his body felt bruised from head to toe. When he clutched the injured arm, he saw droplets of blood falling on the floor, turning sawdust into clumps of red. But as Forrest jumped up on the tilt table and ducked under the mean-looking hook call the dog, Jake raised his good arm to the lever above him. "Don't come near me or I'll pull it," he warned.

"Jake, I'm trying to help you," Forrest said, pausing on the tilt table.

Jake, adrenaline pumping, pulled down on the lever as hard as he could. He wanted to see all the gears go into action. He wanted to force Forrest to retreat. Maybe, in his panic, he even wanted to hurt Forrest for the fright downstairs and for that bruise on Karma's face.

Nothing happened, of course. The lever fell like a broomstick. A quiet slam echoed, and a little dust rose. That's all. What had he expected? The sawmill had been shut down for twenty years. Karma had been kidding about the lever. Jake had known that, hadn't he?

Forrest squatted down beside him, fished a hand-kerchief from his pants pocket, and placed it gently over the wound. The handkerchief turned bright red immediately.

"It needs pressure, Jake," he said as his big hands gripped it gently but firmly. "Hold it like this while I go fetch a first aid kit. Are you hurt anywhere else? That was a nasty fall."

He waited for Jake to put his hand over the wound and then sat back on his heels. "Look, what are you doing here, anyway? This is no place for a kid. Sorry I scared you like that, but I thought you were one of the kids who sneaks in here and steals things." Forrest paused but Jake's mouth still felt too dry to speak.

"Jake, I swear I didn't recognize you until you got to the stairs. You know I'm not going to hurt you, right?"

Jake's pulse was beginning to slow down. Maybe Forrest had mistaken him for a vandal. Anyway, he needed something done about this arm, and probably Forrest knew what to do. "You have a first aid kit?" he ventured.

"If you don't, I do," came a girl's voice. Jake and Forrest both turned as a head of blonde dreadlocks poked up from the stairwell. "I just got it from the sawmill's old office."

"Karma," Jake said happily.

"Are you okay, Karma?" Forrest asked, rising. "How long have you been here?"

Jake detected a note of worry in the last question. He figured Forrest wanted to know if Karma had caught him using the sawmill and dip tank.

"I'm fine. Never mind about me. Jake's arm is bleeding pretty badly," she pointed out. She handed a large, dust-covered case to Forrest.

"Thanks," he said, opening it and pulling out some dressings. "Can you wet one of these in the river for me?"

"Not so sure the river isn't poisoned by your dip tank stuff," she returned, eyes narrowed at him. "Better to use the antiseptic wipes in the kit."

Jake watched Forrest's shoulders slump, but the man said nothing as he pulled out the wipes and began working on Jake's arm. Jake winced at the sting, and then at the increased pressure that Forrest's strong fingers applied while he wrapped some gauze around the arm.

"We left you some more food," Jake said to Karma, smiling.

"I know," she replied, lifting the food pack from behind her. "Want some?"

"Not right now," Jake answered.

"So you were here looking for Karma?" Forrest stated as he finished bandaging Jake's arm. "Is your friend with you too?"

"Peter's gone back to Eagle Lake," Karma replied, standing and crossing her arms as she looked down on Forrest, "probably to report what you've been up to around here, Forrest. Maybe you can tell us exactly what that is."

Forrest sat back on his haunches and gave the two youths a long, defeated look. "I have a little business going making fence posts. It's been helping support the community. It's not legal without a permit, but Bud Olsen—that's the rancher who owns this land," he turned to explain to Jake, "is okay with my doing it as long as I give him a ten percent cut. So yes, you could get me in trouble. Bud too. If that's what you want, Karma."

Karma uncrossed her arms but said nothing.

"Of course, it's not the authorities you want to get me in trouble with. But you can't do any more damage to Skye and me now, not even if you tell her."

"What does that mean?" Karma asked him, lips pursed.

"Skye and I are finished," Forrest said, staring at the floor in front of him. Then he raised steely eyes to Karma. "Just like you've wanted. It was her choice. Plus the community has voted me out. Also like you wanted, Karma. So go ahead and report me to environmental authorities for running a secret business that helped pay the community's bills the last six months."

"Skye called a vote?" Karma ventured.

"It's her right, as leader of the community," Forrest said with bitterness. "And you mean more to her than I do." He paused for a long time. "So go back, Karma. You've made your point, you know. And you don't realize how desperately worried she is. You two'll be fine without me around."

Forrest redirected his gaze to Jake.

"So why were you trying so hard to find Karma?" Jake dared to ask.

Forrest stared at the tilt table. "Thought if I found and returned her, Skye might take me back." His eyes shifted to the big hook. "But she wouldn't have."

The pounding of the rain, the smell of dampened sawdust, filled their corner of the sawmill.

"What's the stuff in the dip tank?" Jake finally broke the silence.

Forrest shrugged and glanced casually toward the tank. "Some wood preservative I found in some old containers in a collapsed shed. Kept costs down, using it up."

"Whose tractor?" Jake dared to ask.

"Bud's. My truck's at his ranch." He emitted a long sigh and rose, avoiding Karma's eyes. "Get that arm double-checked by a doctor," he directed Jake. "And I suggest both of you stay out of this rotting, falling-down place. It's dangerous."

The sadness in his voice was punctuated by an eagle's cry high overhead.

20   Best Tricks

"**L**et 'er rip, Sally! Bust a big one, Dougie! Rock on with Rocky!" Rocky shouted as he accelerated Hoochie's Ride. Jake and Peter smiled as they each gave their new Jet Skis some throttle either side of Hoochie's Ride while pulling students behind them on wakeboards.

Jake couldn't believe Rocky had gone into town one morning and traded in his two two-strokes for the new four-strokes, just like that. But Jake liked how the new Jet Skis handled. They were still louder than the quieted-down Hoochie's Ride, but definitely not as loud and screechy as the old two-strokes.

The two-strokes had been getting pretty old, Jake reasoned. He loved that the new four-stroke Jet Skis went faster than the old ones. Even Skye had grudgingly approved them after Rocky had promised not to run them during next year's pipping season.

Anyway, Jake was having a blast helping his students shred the wake behind him today as Karma, seated in the back of Hoochie's Ride, spotted for Rocky. Two older students were spotting for Jake and Peter. Jake was happy that his arm didn't hurt so much today. Though he hadn't decided to wakeboard today yet, he was the happeningest Jet Ski pilot on Eagle Lake. Well, okay, maybe even with Peter, he thought, glancing over at his buddy, who was neck and neck. Jake did a quick glance behind him to check on Dougie, who'd refused to wakeboard behind anyone else. He watched Dougie cruise up and over the small wake of the Jet Ski and do a surface 180. The kid was coming right along, he thought.

The Wakeup Wakeboard School had a record-breaking twenty-one students today, and the lake conditions were as smooth as butter. The kids were hooting and hollering as they took turns doing tricks for their audience. Their audience consisted of every parent, sister, brother, uncle, aunt, cousin, and neighbor they'd ever had, as far as Jake could tell. It seemed like half of Bellingham had shown up for today's fundraiser. And the kids, many of whom had become regulars over the past two weeks, were doing some pretty impressive tricks for their age and skill level.

Jake watched as a red-haired twelve-year-old tried a "pop." Of course, she started her rotation too soon, before she was fully in the air. But she wore a smile as she waved to her mom after the splash into the lake. Behind Rocky, an older blonde girl did a good-looking wake 360, never mind that she tumbled in after a successful landing. Jake grinned wide as Karma shouted, "Hit it, girl," from her spotter seat.

"She's sure got the jargon down," Skye said with a smile and a roll of her eyes as Jake pulled up to the dock a minute later. She was seated at the end of the dock on a new beach chair Rocky had bought her. She held a block of cedar in her hands. As her knife worked the block deftly, thin, fragrant wood chips floated down to the dock and into the water.

"What're you making?" Jake asked her as he pulled to shore.

Her smile widened as the breeze off Eagle Lake lifted her long blonde hair, then let it settle back gently around her tanned shoulders. "You'll have to wait and see."

"Lunch!" Tao bellowed from the door of the cabin.

"Lunch!" Dougie echoed with gusto as he splashed out of the water.

"Food!" A dozen children took up the chant as wakeboards got put on racks with a clatter, Hoochie's Ride docked, and Tao and some of his commune helpers set trays of food out onto makeshift tables in front of the porch.

Karma leapt out of Hoochie's Ride and gave her mom a quick hug. "Is it going to be an eagle?" she asked, looking at the emerging woodcarving.

"You'll have to wait and see," came the teasing answer.

"Jake!" Karma greeted him. "Rocky says we've already raised more than a grand today. Bud and Forrest will be pretty happy about that."

"That's for sure. It's awesome," Jake agreed. "The Heritage Society has agreed to match whatever we make, right? Guess it'll cost a ton to turn the sawmill into a museum and historic site for tourists."

"Yes, but Forrest has rounded up an army of volunteers to help with repairs," Skye pointed out. "And donations are pouring in back in town, too."

"Did you hear they're going to make Forrest dress up like an old sawmill worker from the 1920s or something when he becomes the head guide there?" Karma asked. "That'll be hysterical."

"I think he'll look like a natural," Tao inserted as he appeared on the dock with a plate of carob brownies. "Better grab one of these before the kids finish them off. Same for the creamcheese-cucumber sandwiches and goat's-cheese quiche."

"Maybe another couple of fundraising days and the sawmill site will have enough money," Skye suggested. She ran a hand over Karma's dreadlocks and inspected a new metal piercing on her daughter's eyebrow. "Think I should get one of those?" she asked with mock seriousness.

"Wouldn't suit you," Karma said, sniffing.

"You're probably right," her mother agreed. "Even if I am the new director of the Eagle Lake Catering Service for The Wakeup Wakeboard School."

"Hey, gang," Rocky addressed the group on the dock. "Did you hear that Bud and Forrest paid their fine and finished draining the dip tank to Environmental Protection Agency specifications? Turns out it was leaking a tiny bit, just enough to hurt some fish in the stream. They said the lake's okay. But some of those fish from the stream washed into the lake and made some of the eagles sick. Anyway, now that the tank's empty, think maybe we should move it down here and have a backyard swimming pool?"

Jake scrunched up his nose. "I hope you're kidding."

"Well, if you believed that lever was going to start up the old mill, I figured you'd fall for that one, too," Rocky ribbed him.

"That tank is now Heritage Society property," Karma reminded Rocky.

"True, and that means anyone who sets foot on the mill site without permission is trespassing. Including the bird blind," Skye spoke up.

"I know, Mom," Karma returned, eyes cast down.

"Hey, Rocky!" Dougie was calling.

"Yes, dude," Rocky replied.

"Everyone wants to see you do a hoochie."

"Today? Now?" Rocky said, resting his hand on Dougie's head. "Well, here's my deal. If Jake and Peter agree to try hoochies for the first time, I'll do you all an other-hand hoochie, which means I have to grab the board with my back hand. It's more difficult than a hoochie."

Whoa, Jake thought. Nothing like putting us on the spot. Neither he nor Peter had tried to pull off a hoochie yet. Still, what the heck. Judging from the way his buddy was looking at him, now was the time, ready or not.

"What's a hoochie?" Skye asked, eyebrows slanting.

"Nothing they can't handle," Rocky egged them on. "Hey, Dougie, go pass the donations can around. Tell everyone that for another fifty dollars total, Jake and Peter will do their first hoochies today or give us one heck of a show trying. And then I'll do my other-hand hoochie."

Dougie leapt up and twirled about in excitement, nearly falling backwards off the dock in the process. "Alright!" he screamed and tore off down the beach.

Jake had seen a few videos on how to prepare for

the trick, and he'd watched Rocky's expert demonstrations, but he dragged his feet a little on the way down the beach.

"It's okay," Rocky assured him. "I've been watching you two and you're ready. Just need to be fully committed and remember to extend your arms all the way. Gravity will do the rest."

"Right," Jake said.

"Yeah!" the kids shouted.

Jake jumped into the water and closed his eyes. He tried to imagine himself flying through the air. In his mind, he did a hoochie over and over, just right. A hoochie. Yes, a hoochie. It couldn't be that hard. As the boat pulled away, he took deep breaths to calm himself. He felt good as he popped up out of the water. He loosened up by doing a few carves between the wake and basked in his students' shouts of encouragement. Soon, he pulled out and set his body position for an approach. As he turned and edged toward the monstrous wake, he burst up and off the lip of the wake. Extend your arms, extend your arms, he reminded himself. He was swinging like a pendulum as he looked at the boat. His throat went dry and he looked down at the water. No! I mustn't look down! But it was too late. He felt the rope lose tension. I'm hooched, he thought. He plunged down face-first into the white foam.

Rocky was quick to swing the boat around and come up alongside him. "Ouch," he called out, face wrinkled with worry.

"You okay?" Peter asked, leaning heavily over the side of the boat.

"Except for making a fool of myself," he responded, forcing a smile. "Entertained 'em, anyway, eh?"

"No worries. Not many get it their first try," Rocky reassured him. "Glad you didn't hurt yourself."

"That was pretty scary!" said Dougie as Jake walked stiffly up the beach. "I thought you got knocked out."

"Nope," Jake said, patting Dougie's head. "I'm tougher than that. And I'm going for it again."

"You sure?" Rocky looked dubious.

"Dead sure," Jake asserted, walking back to the water and wading in.

As Rocky got back into position, Jake signaled him to hit it. Rocky pulled him out of the water once again, grimacing as if uncertain he should've allowed Jake a second go.

Jake shook off the cobwebs and visualized the trick in his mind, this time in slow motion. Once the boat was up to speed, he pulled away from it once again, set his body in position, and turned back toward the wake. With a burst of speed, he popped up off the wake, extended his arms, and flew through the air.

"Superboy," he told himself. As he locked his eyes

on the boat this time, he let go with his lead hand and felt behind him till his fingers touched his board. He could see Karma in the boat cheering him on. He let go of the board and grabbed the handle once again. Then he pushed the handle toward the water and, to his relief, felt his feet come back down underneath him. He knew before his crouched body and angled board hit the lake that he was going to land smoothly, as if he had done this a million times before. He threw the handle and sank down into the lake, smiling from ear to ear as deafening cheers rose from shore.

Fifteen minutes later, Peter, of course, got it first time around, even if he did look a little shaky rising after his landing.

"Awesome, old buddy!" Jake shouted louder than anybody from his spotter position on Hoochie's Ride.

"Thanks for spotting for me," Jake addressed Karma a short while later, as they lined up for food.

She smiled. "Way better entertainment than playing violent video games." She winked at Peter as she accepted a piece of vegetarian quiche from Tao. "And you'll be so much healthier now with our vegetarian catering, you'll forget all about corn dogs."

"I'm willing to forget corn dogs," Peter volunteered, dangling a carrot smothered in artichoke dip over his mouth. He plunked into an easy chair as Jake crawled into the hammock. Both turned to look at Hoochie's grave at the same time.

"Rocky, do you think you'll ever get another dog?" Jake asked quietly.

"I don't know," he responded, looking at Skye. "They chase birds, you know."

"Not this one," Skye said softly with a smile.

Jake, Peter, Karma, and Rocky all looked at her. She fished something out of her pocket and, lifting both hands, held it up to Rocky.

There was silence for a moment except for the sound of Rocky drawing in his breath.

"It's beautiful," Rocky finally said, accepting her carving. Jake twisted in the hammock to get a better look. Sure enough, there was Hoochie, nose up to sniff the air, bandanna flying beside him.

"You're the best," Rocky said, giving Skye a quick hug that she accepted.

"Rock on with Rocky, Jake, and Peter," she said. "Rocky Benson's good times have moved to the Northwest!"

Acknowledgements

My No. 1 helper on this book was Steve Hahn of www.wakeshots.com in Phoenix, Arizona (formerly of Bellingham, Washington). Steve is a wakeboarder, photojournalist, and new dad. He helped me with the wakeboard action scenes while sweating it out waiting for a phone call from his wife to say she'd gone into labor with their first child. The manuscript and the baby developed and arrived at the same time! Thanks also to environmental consultant Tony Kavelaars and his son Chris; veterinarian Fritz Harninghauser of Bellingham, Washington; eagle aficionado and former Forest Service ranger Melanie Peck Graham of Mount Vernon, Washington; and my ever-faithful mechanics consultant, Peter Moffat. Also to my talented new teen editor, Julian Legere.

The staff of McLean Mill, a historical site in Port Alberni, British Columbia, were immensely helpful in giving me a personal tour, answering questions, and reading portions of the book—especially Keith Young, Kirsten Smith, and Neil Malbon. Kudos also to Diane Barrie and the students of Ridgeway Elementary in West Vancouver, British Columbia, for their creative help with providing alternative words for "hippie communes."

Last but not least, thanks to the usual couldn't-do-it-without-you crew: my husband, Steve; my son, Jeremy (lead singer of Jake's and Peter's favorite band, Retrofire); my literary agent Leona Trainer; my editor Carolyn Bateman; my speaking tours agent Chris Patrick; and all the staff of Whitecap Books and Firefly Books.

Look for the next book in the Take It to the Xtreme series, when Jake and Peter do some very unusual BMX biking.

ISBN 978-1-55285-510-2

1

"Up shot the kayak into the air, only to perform a harrowing backflip. Shoved helmet-first into the center of the spinning cocoon, Peter had never felt a force so determined to pry him from his boat. Hanging upside down, gripping his paddle shaft with all his might, Peter waited, counted, and prayed."

Arch rivals and sometimes friends Peter and Jake are delighted to be part of a white-water-rafting trip. But after a series of disasters leaves the group stranded in the wilderness, it's up to them to confront the dangerous rapids to search for help. This is the first title in the extreme outdoor sports series by Pam Withers.

2

Jake, Peter, and Moses are looking forward to heli-skiing and snowboarding in the backcountry near Whistler. But just after they're dropped off on a mountain peak, bad weather closes in and a helicopter crashes. It's up to them to rescue any survivors and overcome avalanches, hypothermia, and wild animals to make their way to safety. This is the second title in the extreme adventure fiction series by Pam Withers.

ISBN 978-1-55285-530-0

It's summer vacation for best friends Peter and Jake, and when they're invited to help develop a mountain-bike trail west of the Canadian Rockies, they can't believe their luck. But as they start working hard in an isolated park, the boys sense that something's not right. Join the boys as they plunge into the mountain biking descent of their lives.

This is the third adrenalin-pumping outdoor sports adventure in the Take It to the Xtreme series.

ISBN 978-1-55285-604-8

Fifteen-year-olds Jake and Peter land jobs as skateboarding stuntboys on a movie set. The boys couldn't be happier, but their dream job proves to be more trouble than they expected. A demanding director, an uneasy relationship with three local skateboarding toughs, and a sabotage attempt—which suggests a jealous rival in their midst—are just some of the obstacles these stuntboys encounter. Coaching from the town's new skate park manager—a former X-Games champ—helps. But after a police chase and an accident that lands someone in the hospital, Jake and Peter know it's time to find out who has it in for them, and why!

ISBN 978-1-55285-647-5

5

Jake and Peter find extreme adventure once again. This time a scuba-diving accident leaves them and a surfer girl stranded on a deserted island with surfboards as their only means of escape. The storm of the century is fast approaching, and the boys need to think fast if they're going to get home in one piece. *Surf Zone* is Jake and Peter's most action-packed, thrilling adventure yet. This adrenalin-pumping book is sure to keep readers on the edge of their seats.

ISBN 978-1-55285-718-2

6

Jake and Peter stumble upon adrenalin-pumping adventure yet again, this time high in the peaks of the Bugaboo Mountains, just west of the Canadian Rockies. Fifteen-year-old Jake is obsessed with solo-climbing a soaring granite spire. His best friend Peter is as absorbed with filming Jake for a video as he is in not divulging his secret fear of heights to the runaway girl who joins them.

Packed with mountaineering lore and cliff-hanging tension, *Vertical Limits,* the sixth in the Take It to the Xtreme series, has competitive gym climbing, outdoor urban climbing, and wilderness rock climbing.

ISBN 978-1-55285-783-0

Take a remote ranch near Spokane, Washington. Add a dirt-bike trail outfitter in need of junior guides. Now stuff the new guides—fifteen-year-old best friends Jake and Peter—in a trailer parked beside the ranch's motocross racetrack. It doesn't hurt, the boys figure, that their boss is a motocross champion willing to coach them and drive them to local races. In fact, it all sounds like a perfect summer for Jake and Peter, who consider themselves the ideal team.

Peter is a freestyle maniac who hates doing bike maintenance. Jake dreams of being a motocross-race mechanic. They ignore warnings from their boss and his fifteen-year-old female ranch-hand that their over-reliance on one another won't work if they're ever separated. It takes a series of race mishaps topped off by a natural disaster to convince them that successful dirt bikers understand their motorcycles inside and out.

ISBN 978-1-55285-804-2

About the Author

Pam Withers is a keen outdoors person who has been involved with many sports. She served as an editor with *Adventure Travel* magazine in Seattle and New York City before doing stints with *The Seattle Times* and *Seattle Post-Intelligencer*. She wrote for publications ranging from *The New York Times* to *McCall's* before working as a book editor and young-adult novelist.

She has been nominated for numerous awards for both her journalistic and fiction writing. She has also found time to race whitewater kayaks, paddle the Colorado River through the Grand Canyon, camp and kayak through northern Russia, and dabble in climbing, skiing, scuba diving, and snowboarding. She speaks to more than 15,000 children across North America per year, as well as at writers' conferences and parents' groups.

Besides the Take It to the Xtreme series, Pam is author of *Camp Wild, Breathless,* and *The Daredevil*

Club. She lives in Vancouver, British Columbia, with her husband and teenage son.

Look for the next book in the Take It to the Xtreme series, when Jake and Peter take up BMX biking. For more information, to write Pam, or to book her for talks, check out www.TakeItToTheXtreme.com.